BLOOD-RED
DEATH

BLOOD-RED
DEATH

MINNA BARDON

COACHWHIP PUBLICATIONS
Greenville, Ohio

For Esther
Who saw the first page first

Blood-Red Death, by Minna Bardon
© 2023 Coachwhip Publications edition
Cover: InstantClipArtOasis license

First published 1947
Minna Bardon, 1900-1974
CoachwhipBooks.com

ISBN 1-61646-561-1
ISBN-13 978-1-61646-561-2

ONE

The atmosphere didn't seem to crackle with suspense. Nobody felt a shiver of murder going by. Everything was a little incredible: the color of the tomatoes, the way the plant was growing from a big tank, the Duchess, and the thin, wildly dancing figure of Uncle Tim waving his fists at the Duchess as she stood near the top of a step ladder grabbing at one of the peach-colored tomatoes.

Anybody would have laughed. The Duchess wore starched red cotton with a sun back and ruffles. She weighed in at some two hundred and sixty-five pounds, if an ounce.

Uncle Tim had originated these new peach-colored tomatoes and was planning to show them at the Hydroponic Fair, and the Duchess was grabbing the best of them, as the Duchess always grabbed everything she wanted. Uncle Tim looked like a small worshipper dancing before a Buddha, except that while he danced he kept shaking his fists at the Duchess and yelling wild imprecations to which she paid not the slightest attention.

Later when they asked me whether she was wearing her diamonds, I thought I remembered the flash of something like dirty rhinestones when she finished eating the tomato and began to tiptoe backwards down the stepladder with all the secrecy of a circus band.

But I wasn't sure of anything except that I had to get back into the kitchen before she came and buttonholed me. I didn't want to have to ask her to stay for dinner, not with her capacity for food and our budget. That's how I missed the fight, if there was one. Uncle Tim claimed that he got away too before she came down from the ladder. "I was afraid I'd kill her," he told the policeman.

I heard a sudden high sharp shriek and almost dropped the casserole I was taking out of the oven, but I got it put down somehow without breakage or burn, and tore out to the kitchen porch to see what was happening.

That's how I happened to be the woman who saw the Duchess die.

Like a palpitating mammoth caparisoned in starched red cotton, she lay there at the foot of the ladder crumpled into a large untidy heap. And then, as I watched, she was quiet.

The Duchess was dead. They asked me later how I knew, so surely, when I was so far away from her, why I didn't run to see if I could do anything to save her life, why I didn't call a doctor or scream for help.

But I knew she was dead. And my feet wouldn't carry me in the direction of the dead woman. Instead, strangely, I found myself going back into the kitchen and moving with horrible quietness between the sink and the stove. I turned off the stove from which I'd taken the casserole, closed the oven door, washed a few dishes, dried them and put them away. But I kept listening, I think, for the scream from outside that would tell me somebody else had found what I had seen.

I came to my senses halfway up the stairs. I suddenly got a good look at my own unconscious cowardice, and sped down to the telephone more quickly than you'd consider possible for a woman of my years and weight.

The police didn't ask as many questions as I'd expected. And they didn't ask me to go out and watch the body while I was waiting for them. Maybe I was a little incoherent at first, because the man on the phone got the notion that I had a drunken husband from whom I wanted protection, but I got the story told, finally, and went back to the kitchen.

In all this time I hadn't seen or heard anybody. I knew they'd ask me what time I'd heard the scream and what time the Duchess had died and I hadn't any notion. I didn't have a watch and there wasn't a clock in the house. It was after three, because I'd listened to the three o'clock news on the radio before I turned it off, and it wasn't more than four, because the stew in the casserole would have been overcooked by four, and it wasn't. That was as close as I could come. The policeman seemed to think it strange that we never knew the exact time, but why should we? Nobody in the house had to make trains or punch any time clocks.

I expected the sounds of sirens or the clanging of bells when the police came, but there wasn't anything like it. Instead, three cars and a sort of ambulance stopped outside and men began getting out. Most of them headed toward the place where the Duchess was lying, just as if I'd told them where to look. I hadn't. But they didn't walk on the grass. They came at her from the side across the gravel path and only one man got real close. The rest of them began to pull things out of what I used to call a mama bag when I used it for baby's diapers. And one man set up, of all things, a camera, and began nonchalantly to take pictures.

That was when I had my first twinge of pity the Duchess. She did so like to have her picture taken, poor old thing. But never like this. She always spent hours in the beauty shop, having facials and hair-dos and manicures, before she sat for a photographer. She had a stereotyped list of expressions she could assume in front of the camera, just as she put on her pearls or her diamonds or the oddly cut garnets she sometimes wore.

"My wistful look?" she suggest. "My dignified look?" I don't know why the whole gamut seemed so funny to me the time I went with her for the session at the photographer's. Now it seemed suddenly tragic to me that a woman who loved to have her picture taken should have the last one when she looked like that.

The kids were about due to come home from the movies and they'd run right into all the mess. But there wasn't any way of getting hold of them and heading them off. After all, seeing the victim of a real murder couldn't be much worse than spending every Saturday afternoon seeing on a screen the exploits of one Bloody Robertson, who'd just as soon shoot you as eat ice cream, as my small son told me gloatingly one day.

A man in a well cut brown suit straightened up and said: "So you're the little woman who phoned about the murder." But he wasn't talking to me. He was almost cooing, in that way that some men use to talk to women, children and lap dogs, and the words were addressed to my next door neighbor, Mrs. Yates.

At the top of her shrill voice, Mrs. Yates was saying, as she came out from behind a tree, "And he killed her, I know he did. He always said he'd kill anybody who stole his old tomatoes—as if we didn't grow some of our own that were much better than his, the old fool."

In my mind I knew that Mrs. Yates hadn't been hiding behind a tree waiting to pounce on the policeman, but it certainly did look that way.

And when she went on explaining that she had seen the body and knew at once that it was murder and who had done it and had called the police, I began to wonder whether I was crazy.

Because I had called the police, after all, not Mrs. Yates, and Uncle Tim hadn't murdered the Duchess because he wasn't the murdering kind, even if he had perfectly good cause for murder.

Just at that moment, Mr. Yates joined his wife. I hadn't seen him come out of the house and cross the yard. But suddenly he was there, as if he'd grown out of the ground like one of the sturdy trees.

He put his hand on his wife's arm and said something to her, in a whisper that I couldn't hear. She turned and looked at him for a minute with her mouth opened. Then she shut up and didn't say another word until the man in the brown suit started his cooing again.

A policeman in uniform came over to the kitchen porch where I was standing about this time and asked: "Who are you?" in a curiously interested sprightly voice, as if my name were an important secret to be learned, before he could go home to dinner.

But the man in brown joined us before I could answer. "I'll take care of the lady, Jones," he said in that cooing voice. "I'm Bradfield of the homicide bureau. And you are . . ."

"I'm Flo Fenton. Mrs. Flo Fenton. This is my house and I called the police and reported the death after I saw the Duches—Mrs. Kelcey Stratton—die."

I felt an odd importance along with my terror. Mr. Bradfield's voice lost a little of its coo. "But that woman down there said she found the body and called the police."

"I gave my name," I told him coldly. "Ask the man I talked to. First he thought I was talking about a drunken husband, but I finally made him understand that it was an accident."

"Accident?" It was funny listening to the coo sharpen into sincerity. "You saw her die? And you say it was an accident?"

I had to tell him off, even if I got the whole homicide bureau down on me.

"A woman of that weight," I told him, "should stay off stepladders. Did you know that more women were killed in their own homes by preventable accidents this years than died in street accidents or in airplane crashes? That fat woman fell off a stepladder and probably broke her neck."

Mr. Bradfield turned to a pale shade of yellow that harmonized with his brown suit. "You saw her fall?" he asked. "Well, there goes our murder case."

"No. But I saw her at the top of the ladder, and I heard her shriek when she saw she was going to fall, and when I came out I saw her lying in a heap at the foot of the ladder, and then I saw her die. It's all very obvious."

"Very obvious," said a cool voice behind me, and I turned to see the tallest man who had ever stepped on my porch. He was at least six and a half feet tall and as thin as the air on the top of a mountain.

"Very obvious," he repeated, "except that the woman did not die from accident. She was murdered—undoubtedly murdered."

"But how—"

"Well," he said thoughtfully, "it might have been the poison, or maybe the fall from the step that was sawed through, or maybe the knife in her back."

"You're joking. Murder isn't anything to joke about."

But the tall thin man shook his head. "I'm not joking," he said. "Three things happened to this woman, all probably within about five minutes. She fell from a step that had been practically sawed through. She took some sort of poison, probably by mouth. And she has a knife, a sharp kitchen knife, in her back."

It was incredible, just as everything else about the whole business was incredible, from the Duchess herself to the peach-colored tomatoes growing on the climbing tree in the concrete tank.

As Uncle Tim came around the corner of the house, I began to laugh and cry at the same time. I simply couldn't help it.

TWO

"This," said the very tall man, "is a new one. I've seen them faint and I've seen them weep. Sometimes they get bopped on the head and sometimes they don't get bopped on the head. But this is the first time I've ever seen this inordinate amount of laughter at the sight of murder."

"I stopped laughing some time ago," I told him with dignity, "and now I'm practically crying."

He looked at me and I didn't blush, much. "I say that you laughed. And it was a little funny," he admitted, "especially the drunken husband that you didn't have."

"You've been talking on the telephone," I accused him, and he nodded.

"Yes. I believe now that you reported the murder. So why did your neighbor, Mrs. So and So, insist that she gave the bad news? And why did your uncle murder the Duchess?"

"My Uncle Tim practically never murders anybody, even Duchesses in red starched cotton dresses with sun backs, poor thing."

And then, all of a sudden, nothing was funny any more. I sat up and I wiped my eyes and wondered how I could have laughed, even if my laughter was mixed with hysterical tears. Because the Duchess was horribly dead and Uncle Tim was probably going to be taken away from his print shop and his garden tank and languish in jail while they heated up the electric chair for him.

In the meantime, Bradfield took him down to the station for some questioning.

And from then on I continued being afraid of everything. For twenty years I had lived down fear, and now suddenly it had come upon me again and I was back in the day when Hugo had been murdered and I had run away.

When I had first seen the Duchess lying there, crumpled into a mammoth heap at the foot of the ladder, I hadn't thought of Hugo. When I thought of Hugo I thought of blood and terror and panic. I thought of myself, twenty years before, young and pretty and crazy with fear, with Hugo's blood smeared all over my hands and on the filmy white chiffon of my wedding dress.

One of the children came home from school one day with a tale of how some insects wall up intruders into the privacy of their honeycombed lives. My secret year was like that. I tucked if away between walls of reticence. I never thought of it, never mentioned it.

It was amnesia of a sort, I guess, but not the kind I pretended it was when I came home from New York after being gone for a whole year without a word.

If Uncle Tim hadn't been the kindest person in the world, if he hadn't completely ignored my silence and welcomed me as if I had been gone an hour, the past twenty years of peace and happiness wouldn't have come to me.

And now I had to keep this thing, this new murder, away from Uncle Tim who couldn't possibly have any connection with it.

The tall man looked down on me, his eyes completely blank and inscrutable. "You've made up your mind," he said. "Can't we get together on this? I've a hunch that you can tell me more than anybody else about the whole thing."

"I know practically everything." I tried to be flippant but the humor died on my lips. "The woman who was killed is the Duchess. We call her that because she looks like one ought to look. She's bigger than I am and probably weighs about two hundred and sixty-five pounds. She's arrogant and disdainful and blunt and if anybody in the world loves her, I don't know who it would be. Everybody from her maid to her banker hates her and you could find enemies anywhere in her world. Her butcher probably sold her poisoned pork chops and her hardware man offered the murderer his choice of knives, free of charge."

The tall man looked down on me. "Very funny. And revealing. And what about you?"

"What about you?" I was really curious.

"My name is G.I. Antwerp. I'm a cop. They call me lieutenant in homicide, but I'm still a cop."

I was willing to believe that. G.I. Antwerp. "They call you G.I., I guess?"

But he shook his head. "They call me Giant. That is a policeman's idea of humor. You may have noticed that I'm tall."

"Must be handy in crowds." The panic was gradually vanishing. The tall man seemed oddly reassuring.

"I specialize in crowds," he said. "I can see now that your Duchess was not a very nice person. But murderers aren't nice, either. You'll help me, Mrs. Fenton?"

His voice was deceptively gentle.. Wasn't there an old fairytale about a giant who had a gentle voice but who killed all his victims: "Fee fi fo fum!"

"I keep remembering how she loved to have her picture taken," I told him. "And they took her picture, out there, with her looking so defenseless."

His nod was brusque but his voice was still gentle. "Death is defenseless."

I thought of Uncle Tim—and of myself, years ago when Hugo was killed and I ran away from murder. "Death is defenseless—but so is life, sometimes. Philosophy while you wait, manufactured by Mrs. Flo Fenton."

He didn't smile. "Mrs. Flo Fenton," he said. "You don't look like a Flo, somehow."

"That belongs back in my show girl days," I told him. "I was Florence when I was young." And then, suddenly, I felt another shiver of fear. He was a detective, after all. And detectives could find out about you. He knew now that I had been a show girl. He could find out that I had been away from home for only one year, that I had come back, apparently suffering from amnesia, unable to answer any questions about my year away from home. That secret year wouldn't be secret much longer, unless I could create some sort of a diversion to get his mind away from any desire to search out my past.

Donny created the diversion, not me. He came home, running even faster than the time the town bully was after him. "Somebody stole my pups and all the tomatoes!" he shouted, and went up the stairs, three steps at a time. He was back again in three minutes, buttoning on the holster that held his strictly useless guns, six-shooters that were carved of wood, painted to represent the real thing.

Giant grabbed at his arm. "Look, kid," he said, "you'd better leave the shooting to us cops. It's our job. You wouldn't want to take our job away from us."

Donny handed over the wooden guns with as much dignity as it they had been real, and the Giant put the guns and their holster and belt on the couch. I remembered it, much later, when I needed it, just as I remembered the flashlight that Donny also took from his pocket and tucked into the pocket of his yellow rubberized raincoat that was lying there on a chair in the dining room.

When Donny and the Giant and I got out to the tomato tank, the thief turned out to be somebody we knew. It was young Junior, son of the Duchess. He was at least thirty, but nobody had ever called him anything but Junior, although his father, Kelcey Stratton Senior, had been dead for years. Junior was a pretty boy, tall and thin, looking much younger than his years, and weaker than anybody would have believed that any man of thirty could be.

He had escaped the Army because of some obscure ailment that didn't prevent him from dancing in a fragile sort of way every night that he could get Natalie or one of the other girls in the neighborhood to join him. No jitterbug stuff for Junior. He floated on the dance floor, no matter what the music and what the rest of the dancers were doing. My sixteen-year-old Tommy called him "Waltz-Me-Around-Again Willie," but he couldn't get the rest of the high school gang to take up the name. Junior had white skin and curly hair and blue eyes. His clothes were just a little too well tailored and his hands waved a little too gracefully to punctuate his conversation. When we caught up with him around the corner of the house, he had a puppy in one hand and a large peach-colored tomato in the other.

He seemed very cheerful, not at all heartbroken because of the murder of his mother, the Duchess.

He handed the puppy to Donny and said: "I was just going to borrow him for a little while to show to Mother. I thought that maybe she'd let me have a pup if she could see how cute it was. And I thought while I was at it, I'd take her one of your Uncle Tim's tomatoes. I knew that you wouldn't mind."

I probably stood there with my mouth open and Donny nearly dropped the puppy.

Was it possible that Junior didn't know that his mother was dead?

The Giant took charge. He said: "Your mother won't be here to object to your having the puppy, if your mother is Mrs. Kelcey Stratton."

Junior laughed shortly. "Won't object? I've been trying to talk her into letting me have a dog for the last twenty-five years. This is as far as I get. I pick out the dog and she says 'no!' Very simple."

"Your mother is not at home." The Giant sounded kindly impersonal.

Junior quirked up the penciled eyebrows on his pretty face. "And what would you know about it?"

"Your mother is dead."

I was ashamed to look at the naked emotions that raced across Junior's face. Incredulous joy. Incredible relief. And then he blanked out every emotion and looked dazed and bewildered. "I don't believe you. I saw my mother a couple of hours ago, right here in this very yard. She was perfectly all right then."

"When? Exactly what time?"

"At about three forty-five. She was on her way to see Mr. Timothy Fenton. I talked to her at least fifteen minutes and then went on downtown."

Looking at his face, I would have known that he lied, even if I hadn't been certain that he couldn't have been there at that time. I'd have seen him or heard him myself—and I hadn't seen Junior.

THREE

I seemed to be drifting through a cloud and the cloud was heavy and cold with fear. Somewhere I knew there was a cruel blaze of light, but I couldn't see it. And then I woke up to the knowledge that I was all alone in the house except for the children. The room wasn't quite dark. I could see the tall shadow of the chest of drawers rising across the room from my bed, and I could see the flicker of a light appearing and disappearing, as if somebody, somewhere, were flashing a signal from afar.

Then, all in a moment, I was completely awake and very hot with anger again.

Strange that murder should make me more furious than afraid. I was in a perfect fury that the Duchess should have been murdered, that Uncle Tim should have been arrested, that the tall giant of a police man shouldn't have believed me.

And just at that moment, I heard a small voice say from the doorway: "Mom, I'm hungry."

It wasn't a surprise. The children had come home to so much excitement after their movie that the supper had been neglected except for the coffee and pie that the Giant had managed to engulf.

Donny always got hungry at midnight, like a man on a morning newspaper, Uncle Tim used to say, remembering his own days on the *Journal*.

19

By the time the light was on and I'd limped down the stairs in bedroom slippers and housecoat, the other boy, Tommy, and we were on our way to the kitchen.

We were sitting at the table when Junior came to the kitchen door. He was even whiter than usual and there was a scratch on his face. His curly hair was mussed and a little muddy as if he had been wallowing in a mudhole, but Junior wasn't a mudhole sort of person and besides, he was a little old for Commando games. He held his left arm oddly and when I opened the door I could see that he was swaying a little.

I let him come in and fixed him a cup of coffee. Donny and Tommy went on with their bread and butter like somebody out of Goethe, wasn't it?

"You've got to help me, Mrs. Fenton," Junior said finally, almost in a whisper.

"How'd you get here, Junior?" Donny talked with his mouth full of bread and butter.

"I got away when they let me go upstairs to get some things I needed. I got down the drainpipe from the bathroom. That's the way I always get out when Mother says I've got to go to bed early. You've got to help me. You don't think I murdered her, do you?" The whisper had become a whine and for the first time, looking at him, I saw something that might be guilt.

I looked at the thin white hands, soft and dirty and much too jittery for the hands of a man of thirty. Could they be the hands of a murderer? But then I remembered my own hands, on that night when I had come home, an hour after my marriage to Hugo, to find him lying in his blood on the floor of my room. I remembered the smear of blood on my hand as I tried to help him, before I realized that my husband of a few hours was dead.

And because I knew that I had been innocent although I'd looked guilty, I took another look at this man who had hated his mother and decided to help him.

I turned on Donny and Tommy. "Get upstairs, kids," I ordered. My usually disobedient offspring know that when I have one certain note in my voice I am "She-Who-Must-Be-Obeyed." I was S.W.M.B.O. at that moment and Donny and Tommy knew it.

They each grabbed a handful of cookies as they went up and I knew there would be a trail of crumbs up the stairs to clean up in the morning, but there are times when privacy is a jewel to be purchased at a good price.

I got the story out of Junior between sobs and hysterics—his, not mine. The police were going to "detain" him. They didn't say "arrest" him. They didn't even say that he was being charged with murder. He hadn't been warned that whatever he said would be used against him.

He had only been asked, in a perfectly friendly fashion, to come down to the police station with the Giant and Bradfield, to answer some questions. "And if I lie," Junior told me, "they'll know it, because I never could tell a lie. And if I tell the truth they'll know I hated my mother. Besides, I—I tried."

Looking at his weak face with that secret look of rather smug prettiness in spite of his tears and mud and hysterics, I wasn't so sure about the lying. I had known Junior to tell barefaced lies and brazen them out. "What did you try, Junior?" I asked.

"I tried to kill her," he said. "I poisoned her. But I used too much and she got over it. She never let me forget. And if I didn't kill her, it wasn't my fault. God knows I tried to be free of her."

For the first time I saw in him a grown man, prisoner to a possessive mother who could have had him clapped into prison at any time he tried to escape. But somehow I didn't have much sympathy left for Junior.

I kept thinking of the Duchess, crumpled into that mammoth heap at the foot of the ladder.

My eyes were unfriendly when I turned to him. "What do you want me to do—help you get away? And where would you go?"

"I have plans," he said with dignity. "I have a place. I got away once before. And Mother never found the place. It is still there, waiting for me."

"Where is it?" But his face closed down on its secret. It became blank, like a bad photograph of itself, and realized that Junior could keep his secrets as well as I.

And in that moment, seeing his secretive face, knowing the hatred that could look out of those pale blue eyes, watching the penciled eyebrows stiffen to determination, I was suddenly afraid of Junior Stratton.

I knew that murder was not beyond him. I knew that he could easily have killed his mother and would just as easily kill me or anybody else who tried to prevent him from going away.

"I want money—I need a hundred dollars. Your Uncle Tim always keeps money in the little secret drawer of the secretary. Get it for me."

He was right. That secret drawer was as secret as drawers ever are in Grand Rapids secretaries turned out by the thousands to pattern. There were at least five in town just like ours, with the same kind of secret drawer in the same place.

"I can't take Uncle Tim's money."

"You'll take it or else—" He got up from the table and came toward me, and there was something about the way his overlong overslim fingers curved that made me back away from him toward the dining room door.

"Don't scream for the boys or the police," he said, with that quietly hysterical desperation that I thought happened only on the stage of stock companies, "or I'll strangle you before they get to you."

He meant it, too. "I'll get it." I backed toward the dining room. I was stumbling past the couch on my way to the secretary when I remembered the guns, the wooden ones, that the Giant had taken from Donny and left on the couch. It was easy enough to seem to trip over the edge of the couch in the half-light that came from the open kitchen door, and when I came up I had a painted gun in my hand and the other gun and holster were tucked under a pillow so Junior couldn't tell what they were.

God knows where I got the melodrama that I used when I said, "Hands up." Donny and Tommy would have been proud of me. I was almost as good as Bloody Robertson, their favorite movie serial villain.

But I hope that I never again see the desperation in a man's eyes that I saw in Junior's, when he obeyed and let himself be ushered back out of the kitchen door.

"You're going to let me go?" Incredulously he looked at me.

"Yes. I'll call the police when you have gone, but I can't hold you now, even with the gun."

I felt as empty as a box of candy half an hour after Donny and Tommy have been turned loose on it, and my knees were as limp as cooked spaghetti. I let Junior run down the walk and even then didn't have the strength to get up and call the police.

I was still holding the gun when Donny and Tommy crept down the stairs again to see what was happening. And just at that moment the Giant walked into the kitchen, by the open door, with a casserole in his hand.

FOUR

Something jogged my memory as I looked at the casserole. It was small and sickly pink with a few anemic blue forget-me-nots painted faintly upon it in a meagre garland.

The Giant's eyebrows lifted as he held the thing toward me.

"That's not mine." My voice wasn't as indignant as I felt. Even a policeman ought to have known that I wouldn't cook in a casserole like that. It would make me seasick.

The giant lifted the lid of the casserole. Inside was an unsightly mess that bubbled up into an ungodly smell. The Giant put the lid back on, quickly. "The tomatoes," he said, "were the color of peaches, like your uncle's. Didn't you say that the tomatoes ripe today were the first you've had?"

The stink still lingered in the air and I went quickly to open the other window wide. I'd waited too long to get my airy kitchen to let it be contaminated with a smell like that.

A quick flash of memory guided my words: "They disappeared," I found myself saying slowly. "There were peach-colored tomatoes about ten days ago. And then they disappeared. We thought some boys, or the Duchess—"

"And then your uncle, thinking that the Duchess had stolen his tomatoes, said that some day he'd murder her if she didn't quit stealing his stuff."

25

"The woman next door told you?" The Giant nodded.

"This is a strangely culinary murder," he said.

"All conferences held in the kitchen," I agreed. "We're thinking of suggesting that the homicide squad move up here for convenience. Coffee served every hour on the hour and scrambled eggs at eight in the morning."

"Do you always eat at midnight? And who was your visitor?"

The Giant sat down at the table and the boys, obeying me, a little to my astonishment, went upstairs to their own rooms when I pointed unmistakably in that direction.

"Always. And my visitor was Junior Stratton."

"Playing guns?" He nodded his head at the wooden gun and I knew that he remembered it.

"Yes. I chased him out of the house at the point of the gun. I was going to call you as soon as I had knees instead of elbow macaroni."

"He threatened you?"

"Yes. He wanted money." I went on to tell him what had happened, and he filled in the gaps.

"Nobody thought he was guilty. We just wanted to know a few things. After all the evidence points to Timothy Fenton as the murderer. Now I'm not so sure."

"Timothy Fenton is no murderer. My Uncle Tim is the kindest man in the world."

To my amazement he agreed with me. "He is a very kindly old man. But he has no illusions. He is a skeptic of the first water. He will do anything he feels needs doing without any sentimentality about it."

"Does that make him a murderer? Murderers are crazy. And Uncle Tim is the sanest person I know."

"He can be absolutely sane on every other thing in the world and yet be a murderer because his logic insists that the world is a better place without some one person whom he then proceeds to murder. I've known other murderers like that."

The house was very quiet. Outside, I could hear somebody moving around, and upstairs the boys were scuffling a little before giving up and getting back into bed.

We sat there, drinking our coffee. I found myself conscious of the housecoat I had thrown on over my nightgown, my face innocent of makeup, my hair tied back with a top string that Donny had left on the table.

I found myself sighing a little. "It's been a horrible day. Even before the murder it was one of my bad days."

"Tell me about it." The Giant's voice was gentle. He stirred his coffee and took a fourth spoonful of sugar.

The day started with fireworks, at six in the morning. "Uncle Tim got up and went down the steps and out to the tomato tank, swearing at the top of his voice. He said that thieves from the Blanketty Blank Hydroponics Club were sabotaging his tomatoes to keep him from revolutionizing the farm methods of the world."

"Did he catch the thieves?"

"That's what's funny. When he got there, every tomato was there. He knew exactly how many he had. About ten days ago, as I told you, some tomatoes were stolen."

"Was that bad?"

"Very bad. Uncle Tim had a formula, Mr. Antwerp."

"Call me Giant. Everybody does."

I told him then about hydroponic farming, as Uncle Tim had explained it to me. "You take a concrete tank and fill it with gravel and sand plus a certain amount of what Uncle Tim calls litter. Then you concoct a nutritive formula out of chemicals and the plants grow."

"What is a nutritive formula? And what chemicals? Poison?"

My answers were more feeble than usual. I told him that the plants grew much faster and bigger than in a field.

I told about how American troops during the war, had grown food on volcanic islands where not even a blade of grass had grown. I told about Uncle Tim's new chemical formula, but I couldn't tell what it was, because I didn't know. I told about the new color of the peach-colored tomato that Uncle Tim had developed, and the way he said that anybody could eat it, even people usually allergic to tomatoes.

"It's going to revolutionize farming," I finished, with triumph and an amazing yawn. I suddenly realized that I had had very little sleep in the last twenty-four hours, and there I was, sitting in a kitchen with a strange man, at some time after midnight.

Just at that minute, in the middle of the yawn, I heard the shot.

I was scared. I found my yawn turning to a sort of stammer as I heard myself saying: "That—that wasn't Donny's gun."

But the Giant didn't waste time on me. And my time was taken up with Donny and Tommy, who were back downstairs in no time flat. I had to keep them in the house by wild threats that we all knew were impossible to carry out.

Bradfield, the homicide man with the cooing voice, stuck his head in at the kitchen door to ask if we had seen the Giant, and Mrs. Yates screeched at the top of her voice: "Flo! Flo Fenton! What are you doing out there now?"

I opened the side window that faced her house and we stood there for a minute, shivering a little with excitement and—on my part, at least—fear. She was sure that we were all going to be murdered in our beds but didn't mention how, since all of us were presumably out of bed.

Mrs. Yates had her hair up in curlers—I always knew that her curls weren't natural—and her voice was even shriller than usual. She was pretty, though, in a skinny sort of way, even without makeup and with her hair not fixed.

"Who got shot?" yelled Tommy out of an upstairs window.

"Somebody said it was Junior—Junior Stratton," Mr. Yates' voice boomed out behind his wife's shoulder. He said something else, to her, under his breath, and she went in and closed the window and I figured I might as well go back to bed, too.

Even if the police had shot Junior, there wasn't anything I could do about it. And poor Uncle Tim was in jail and would have to stay there until we found the real murderer.

I put away the things in the kitchen, turned out the lights and went up to bed, firmly discouraging the boys' desire for excited conversation.

I had earned my rest.

I fell asleep with a strange feeling that there was something important about the Duchess that I'd have to remember to tell the Giant the first thing in the morning.

FIVE

A woman's scream slashed out against the darkness of the night. I found myself trembling as I went to the telephone. And then I realized that it wasn't my affair, this time. Uncle Tim was safe in jail and my children were safe upstairs in their beds and there wasn't anything I could do to help the woman who had screamed—even if I did call the police.

The children didn't awake. I got upstairs, somehow, on trembling feet, and stood for a moment in the door of their bedroom, looking at them in the faint spotlight from the hall lamp.

A sleeping child is at the same time so young and so defenseless. Even Donny, the tough, was a gentle baby, sleeping with his rumpled curls hovering above his serene brow.

A middle-aged fat sentimentalist, I called myself as I went back downstairs and picked out a less gory book for my solitary entertainment. I hadn't read even two pages, and wasn't any too sure about the words on those, when the doorbell rang sharply.

Reluctantly I got to the door and peered out through the glass before I unfastened the chain. The Giant was there, standing impatiently on one leg and then the other like a stork readying himself for a marathon race.

He came in and slammed the door behind him so hard that I hoped the children hadn't awakened. "You're all right? Did you scream?"

"I never scream on Wednesdays." I was amazed that I could still be flippant with poor Uncle Tim there in jail and piercing screams rending the air.

He looked at the book in my hand. "Good Lord, woman, after all you've gone through tonight, surely you don't need to read yourself to sleep. Are you Superwoman?"

I felt no fear any more and not even any sleepiness. I felt excited and eager. "Look," I said, "we're going to do something. I'm going to help you find that murderer. I want my Uncle Tim to come home."

The Giant looked down on me and I saw the twitch of a smile at the corner of his mouth. I guess it was a little funny. It was his job to go hunting murderers. "You probably find twenty killers every day and twenty-five on Sunday," I apologized, "but this one is very important to me, because of my uncle."

"Every murder is important to people who love the victim or the suspects. And you're right about one thing. Murder is my job. It's a dirty job. You uncover sewers of emotions, plenty of dirt. You work overtime and you lose sleep. And you wouldn't give it up if somebody offered you a million dollars and a mansion in the clouds."

Looking up at him, I could see that he meant every word. "You've worked all night?"

He nodded. "I went on at four, and it's hours later now. I was going back to my place and go to sleep, but that scream stopped my plans. If you're all right I'll go on. Good morning."

I was asleep as soon as my head touched the pillow, and so it wasn't until the next morning that I knew about the second death.

This time it was Mr. Yates.

Tommy told me when I dragged down to the kitchen and got my coffee started. I'm not half human in the morning until I've had my coffee, especially when I've had only a little sleep.

The rest of the day was as glum as any day I'd ever spent. It wasn't exciting—it was sordid. I couldn't tell anybody anything. They asked me time and time again about what happened when Mr. Yates spoke to his wife and she closed the window.

I couldn't tell whether they seemed to be quarreling. I didn't know whether she had screamed. I didn't seem to know much of anything, except what they told me, that Mr. Yates was dead.

I didn't like Mrs. Yates, but when I saw her tear-ravaged face, pity rose in me. I, too, had lost my husband by murder. I wanted to tell her, but of course I couldn't. A secret that is kept for twenty years must be kept forever if lives are not to be destroyed.

I didn't think of Thompson Fenton as my husband. He was the man I had married a year after I came back. He was the father of my children, and I hadn't seen him since the day Donny was born.

He had come into the hospital where I lay with my baby and had looked down on me and the boy. "Well, Flo," he'd said, "I'm off. I've had enough of the life domestic. I think I'll try Alaska."

That was the last word I'd heard from him—not a letter or a wire, nothing. I'd known almost from the beginning that it would be like that with Thompson Fenton. The silent showgirl with pretended amnesia fascinated him when I first went back to Uncle Tim. Thompson Fenton was Uncle Tim's nephew, too, on the other side of the family. Uncle Tim was so happy when Thompson and I told him we were to be married.

But when I reverted to the domestic, I lost my fatal fascination for Thompson. He had liked the baby, then Tommy; but soon grew tired of him. "I'm not the father type," he told me when I showed him the new baby, Donny.

Hugo had been my husband—the man I loved. He was older than I, a dashing young man with a mocking quirk to his eyebrows and a knowing cynicism around his mouth. He'd loved me and he'd married me, although there were at least two other women in his life. I hadn't waited to find out which of them murdered him because all the clues were laid so that I myself seemed to be the murderer. When I saw my bridal veil stained with his blood and the marriage license crushed under his body with the note from another woman, I had known that the only way I'd get away would be to go quickly.

I kept wanting to tell Mr. Yates how I felt, but I couldn't. I baked cakes and took one over to her, and she said through her tears: "You shouldn't have bothered, Flo. I never eat cake—my waistline, you know. And chocolate isn't good for my complexion."

She went back to the tears afterwards, and I walked out of her house with an insane desire to slam the door after me.

I found Donny scraping the bowl from the cake batter and got back to normal again by the time the kitchen looked as usual. I went out with Donny to play with the puppies and that was how I found the gun.

A couple of the puppies were nosing around something made of dark metal, and I thought at first that it was one of Donny's painted guns.

But this time it was the real thing. I knew that clues ought to be left for the police and yet I didn't want one of the boys to pick up a loaded gun and get shot, so I upturned the new garbage pail over it and warned Donny to stay on the other side of the house.

There was a policeman in uniform standing on the porch of the Yates house, and I called him and told him what I'd found. He seemed to find the upturned garbage can funny.

Bradfield, the detective with the brown suit and the cooing voice, came and thanked me for finding the gun. "We looked over every inch of your place and the Yates' this morning," he said. "I went over that dog pen myself, and I know the gun wasn't there half an hour ago."

"The pups could have carried it, maybe?" Donny put in hopefully.

"Ix-nay. The pups can't carry even a bone. Besides, the gun was probably loaded. It would have gone off and blown the pups to pieces if they'd try to lift it," countered Tommy.

But Donny was sure of his facts. "Buster has a dog he trains to carty newspapers, and a newspaper is bigger than a gun."

"But not so heavy." We left them arguing about the possibilities while the detective brought me up to date on the murders.

Uncle Tim hadn't exactly been charged with murder. He was just detained as a material witness, whatever that was.

Mr. Yates had been shot, probably with the gun I'd found. He had been found by his wife, lying on the floor of their living room with a bullet in his heart. It was her scream that I'd heard in the night.

"Maybe they'll realize now that Uncle Tim didn't murder the Duchess. There couldn't be two murderers on one street, could there?"

Bradfield looked at me. "There may not be a murder this time," he said. "It looks like suicide, except that the gun was gone. And somebody said that the wife might have thrown the gun away so it would look like murder instead of suicide."

The cooing voice didn't sound a bit illogical, although the facts did. "Why should Mrs. Yates want to have people think that her husband was murdered if he really committed suicide? And why should he commit suicide?" It was none of my business, but I wanted to know.

Gently the detective mentioned to me that some insurance policies paid in case of murder but did not pay for suicides. And Mrs. Yates would want to have the insurance paid.

"But why would he kill himself?"

"Things were bad. He had taken money to pay bills that his wife had run up. The Duchess—Mrs. Stratton—found it out and exposed him. He had plenty of reason for suicide."

"And a darned good reason for killing Mrs. Stratton," I suggested, suddenly very hopeful for Uncle Tim.

But the cooing voice demurred. "He was closeted with his boss all yesterday afternoon, getting the devil because of what he had done. They just let him go home to put his affairs in order before they clamped down on him more today."

"He came home to a lot of peace and comfort, didn't he?" I kept thinking of Mr. Yates' face the day before when he'd come home to find his wife standing over the body of the Duchess; remembering the man's voice the previous night when he had said that Junior Stratton had been shot.

How had he known? I asked Bradfield: "Did something happen to Junior—to young Kelcey Stratton?"

"Nothing that I know of. We asked him a few questions and sent him home. He's probably curled up in his feather-bed sleeping the sleep of the bachelor."

So Junior hadn't been shot? But it was a shot we heard. Even I knew that. And Mr. Yates had been perfectly all right at that time. I kept wondering about it all that day, and as I shut my eyes that night, the problem still troubled me.

SIX

I woke up again at about midnight, thinking I heard a noise. I went downstairs. I heard a scrap of paper rustle somewhere in the kitchen as if a mouse were scuttling into a dark corner. But I hadn't seen a mouse in that kitchen since the new floor was laid four years before.

I fumbled for the light switch and pressed the button, but nothing happened. The lights were gone. But they were all right in the rest of the house. No fuse had blown out. Maybe the bulb was done for. But it was almost a new bulb. I'd put it in only a couple of days before.

Donny's flashlight was in the pocket of his raincoat. I got back into the dining room, grabbed the raincoat, found the flashlight and was back in the kitchen before I began to figure out that I should be afraid in the dark, so soon after murder, with the murderer loose somewhere in the neighborhood.

Was I going to be one of those dreadful females who went around being bopped on the head by murderers? I had always detested them and the Giant's disdain hadn't helped my opinion.

I found the light. The bulb was loose in the socket, nothing worse. I was just about ready to turn it when something fell on my foot and I started to swear with the vocabulary of the mother of any small boy. I saw stars for a minute. Nobody had ever told me that the stars you see are purple with white points. I heard somebody and I felt the small breeze of somebody dashing past me, and then I was alone in the dark. Alone, but without the bop on the head that I had considered inevitable. Somebody had come into my house and had gone out again, probably by the open kitchen window.

I got the light on finally, and this time I didn't need any urging to call the Giant.

But a stranger with a bored voice answered the phone. "We'll see about it. Want a policeman now? Sure it wasn't a dog or a cat?"

"I don't know any dogs or cats who know how to turn off light bulbs." I gave my name and address, and the bored voice brightened considerably.

"Look, that's where the two murders were, or the murder and suicide. I'll get somebody up there right away."

By that time I was mad. "You needn't bother," I said with dignity. "But you'd better have your police do a better job of patrolling this neighborhood or somebody else will be murdered soon—maybe one of the policemen, if he comes too late after he's called."

I roused Tommy and we went through the house, turning on every light, and couldn't find anything. Somebody had been raiding the icebox and had taken the new fruitcake that I'd baked and put away, as well as some sliced meat that was left over from supper. The rest of the loaf of bread was gone, too, and my vacuum bottle was missing and some coffee that had been left in the pot on the stove. From the aroma in the kitchen, I knew that somebody had been heating up the coffee.

A couple of policemen in uniform got there just about as we finished. We told them what we had found and they went over the house with us again. By that time Donny was stirring restlessly and Tommy was yawning every three minutes, so we got rid of the police as soon as possible. They asked whether we wanted a guard of some kind in the house, but by that time I wasn't much afraid any more and we said good-bye and the policemen left. They may have stayed around outside the rest of the night, I wouldn't know. I was asleep in five minutes and was still asleep the next morning when Thompson came home.

Thompson Fenton looked older, much older. I hadn't seen him since the day Donny was born. Then I had been in bed at the hospital with my new baby. Now I was in bed in my own room, waking up from some horribly real dreams about the ways that Junior might have murdered his mother and Mr. Yates and be planning to murder me.

"Repeat performance," said Thompson. "Another baby? And who is the father this time?"

I wasn't more than half awake, I guess, because I didn't feel the instant fury that the sight of him would have brought to me at any other time.

I blinked open my eyes and then closed them again. "Go 'way. You're a bad dream."

Thompson laughed. "So this is how my ever-lovin' wife feels. I'd better go back to Alaska and points north." He sat down on the edge of the bed and looked at me quizzically. "Not a bad-looking gal, even if you are fair, fat and forty," he said. "Did you ever divorce me? I never thought to ask."

"No. I'm still married to you, but that's because you saved me from other men. I was through with them, after you. Except Uncle Tim and the boys."

"Where's the old fellow?"

"In jail."

Thompson guffawed. "What did he do? Kill somebody or rob a bank to get cash for his garden? I always did think he was too good to be true."

Knowing that I looked my worst, I found it very easy to wonder why on earth I'd ever married him. Thank goodness neither of the boys looked or acted anything like him.

"He's accused of a murder he didn't do. And if you'll please get out of my room, I'll go down and start breakfast."

I scrubbed myself to cleanliness, hating myself and my looks. After all, I was fair, fat and forty, and even if I cared nothing about Thompson now, he was my husband and the father of my children.

I had breakfast on the table by the time the boys came down. I hadn't had a chance to break the news to them when Thompson came in and seated himself at the breakfast table.

"Hi, there, boys," he said. "Let me introduce your father."

Donny and Tommy looked at him wordlessly. Then Tommy got up and went over to stand beside Thompson. "Look," he said, "come outside with me, will you? I've always wanted to punch your block off and this a good time to start."

I hadn't known that Tommy felt that way. He must have been harboring resentment against his father for a long time to collect storm clouds like that. But Thompson just laughed.

"Sit down and keep your shirt on, kid. We'll fight as much as you like later. I'd like some of your mother's coffee first."

And the rest of the morning was like that. No fights. No explanations. Just matter of fact unemotional talk, as if he had walked out of the house an hour before. No questions and no answers. He just slipped out from under everything.

There was a certain magnificence in his indifference. He wanted to do something and he did it without regard to the consequences. If he met Natalie, he would probably make love to her in the same off-hand way, disregarding the fact that she was Junior's pet girl friend.

For Natalie was just the kind of girl that Thompson liked. She was one of those predatory young females who might be any age from eighteen to thirty-eight. Thin, medium height, dyed hair with a permanent and some rather conventional ringlets at shoulder length, clothes a little too closely fitted, heels too high, new nylon stockings, high makeup, bright long toenails and fingernails to match.

While I was getting dressed to go to see Uncle Tim, Thompson left again, with a casual word to the boys, and none at all to me, and I woke up to the terror of the whole thing.

Was it only a coincidence that Thompson had come back now, at this time of danger to the family? I doubted it.

I was just about dressed and had the door opened, when I saw the Giant coming up the walk.

Suddenly fear swept over me.

SEVEN

"You look sick and lonely," said the Giant. "But it's more than that. "You're scared."

I nodded. "I'm ashamed of it," I agreed, "but I am scared. I was never so frightened in my life. I'd like to take my children and flee with them over the ice to the mountains or some place, so far away from murder that I'd never hear the word again."

"You can't run away from murder."

"Oh, but I can. I know." I thought of the secret year of my life, and all that had happened.

The Giant shook his head. "You can't run away from murder. Or from fear, Mrs. Kiphart."

"So you know." My secret year was no longer a secret.

There was pity in the eyes of the tall thin man, but his words were relentless. "It was very easy," he said. "Everything about this case is easy and simple and obvious. Your Uncle Tim hated the Duchess. To make things worse she was threatening to tell everybody who you were. And then when she stole the tomatoes, that was the last straw. Your Uncle Tim killed her and you knew it. Maybe you had a hand in the murder too."

Outside, the children played in the yard with the puppies; I could hear them laughing and shouting. And inside

43

the house, the life I had built for them and myself was shattered into bits.

"How long have you known?" I hardly knew my own voice.

"I was sure of my facts this morning. I came directly to you."

"But Uncle Tim didn't murder her. And she didn't know. She couldn't have known. I didn't know myself, until just a short time ago," I lied.

"Is that the truth? Somehow I find it very difficult to believe in all the amnesia cases we hear about."

I felt the blood rush to my face. My muscles tightened as if I were gathering strength to run away. It had been hard to keep the fiction of my amnesia all those years. Maybe nobody else believed in it, any more than the Giant did. But nobody else knew my connection with Hugo. The Giant's words proved that he did.

My legs wouldn't hold me and I groped my way to a chair and sat down. The Giant sat down too. "Tell me all about it," he said gently.

The words came slowly after the long silence. "Nobody knew who I was except Hugo, and he didn't tell. I was a show girl and Hugo told me that I'd be more interesting to the producer as a sort of mystery girl. I was pretty, in a tall sort of show girl way, and Hugo taught me tricks of walking and standing and talking that made me seem exotic. That was twenty years ago, please remember."

"I see." His eyes were glazed with thought.

"Nobody knew where I came from. They thought I was a European. I let little things drop. Hugo taught me how to speak with a sort of accent that some folks considered fascinating." I stopped, remembering for a moment the heady intoxication of the girl I had been, twenty years before, turned loose in the world of the would-be Bohemians. We were young enough to consider Greenwich

Village dramatic and wonderful instead of just one more slum district in a big city. We dramatized ourselves and each other. We were very young—young enough to believe in the "Flaming Youth" that F. Scott Fitzgerald gave us.

"Hugo was your husband, Hugo Kiphart—the one who was murdered?"

"He wasn't my husband then. He was just a man I met the first week I went to New York. A year later he married me. And that same day he died."

"He was murdered." The Giant's voice was emotionless. "Did you kill him?"

"No. But I ran away because I was afraid to stay. I still don't understand why the police didn't find me."

"I have looked up the records. The police thought that the wife was a certain European who fled to South America and was never heard from again. The case is closed, as much as any case is ever closed if there is a murderer at large."

"Did you tell them? Are they coming to get me?" With panic I thought of my children. What would they become if they were left to Thompson? What could I do? For twenty years, this had been my nightmare. Now it had happened.

"No. I have told them nothing. I have asked questions without saying much. I wanted to be sure."

"But you can be sure. I didn't kill him. I couldn't have killed him. Mr. Antwerp—Giant—I was a girl, a very young girl, very much in love with a fascinating older man. I was a little fool to marry him, knowing nothing about him, but I did. Then I had a wire, on my wedding day. I thought that I was going to meet my husband. But he didn't meet me. And when I got back to the hotel, there he was, on the floor of my room, killed."

The Giant sat up straight. He stood up and walked over to me, towering above me like an ogre on a pedestal.

"To meet your husband? But hadn't you just been married?" he asked.

I remembered. The memories came back in a rush. "He had to leave me at the hotel immediately after the ceremony. I was to join him later. Then I had this wire to join him at the Waldorf—and I waited but he didn't come. So I went back and found him."

In the silence memory grew and I saw again the face of my darling, with a streak of blood across his forehead, his eyes staring at me with terrible vacuous finality.

And yet there was a certain relief in telling it. "I—I guess I should have stayed. But it was so hopeless, and I was so very young. My wedding veil was crushed under his body and stained with his blood. My marriage license was bloody, and so was the letter. It was open, so I could read every word, but there was blood across the margin, just where she had written, 'Hugo, my darling!'"

I knew again at that moment the agony of the discovery. "It was a love letter? From another woman?" insisted the Giant.

Out of the misery of the past, I nodded. "She loved him, and he had loved her. He was going to see her. He told her he was marrying me because I was young and he didn't want to hurt me by throwing me over, but he really loved her."

"All of it was in the letter?"

I nodded my head that was heavy with the pain of twenty years. "She told him how happy it made her to hear him say those things to her. She said them over and over, all the way down the bloodstained page."

"Did you touch the letter? Was your name on the license?"

"I didn't touch the letter. I didn't have to. It was lying there for me to read when I knelt there beside him to try to save him." Pain was sharp and shining. It gave me back my youth, and for a moment Hugo was alive and beloved, for me.

"And the license? Your name?"

"I used my theatrical name, Maria Thomassen. Hugo told me to. He named me."

"That was why you were never traced here. There was a real Maria Thomassen. She was the woman who wrote the letter. She was the woman who went to South America and was never traced."

"But why should they think that she wrote the letter if she married him?" He shrugged his shoulders. The silence in the room was alive. There were no words any longer. There were no sounds except the whimpering of the puppies outside.

In all of that time I had not thought of Thompson and his strange arrival. It wasn't until he appeared at the door and stood there grinning that I realized he was on earth.

He came in, offering his studied charm, like a routine gift of flowers or candy.

"Mr. Antwerp," I found myself saying, "this is Thompson Fenton, my husband."

This time the Giant stood straight up, towering above Thompson's head. "But I thought that you were a widow," he said bluntly.

Thompson laughed. "She is, more or less," he said. "I walked out on her when the kids got too much for me, and I walked back just to see what was going on. Maybe we ought to get a divorce, so we'll be free for further excitement in the marital field."

The Giant looked him up and looked him down and turned toward the window without a word. Thompson went on talking: "So you've got the old man in jail. Did he kill the old girl?"

"I don't know," the Giant said slowly.

"How'd you come to arrest him? The boys didn't know, when I asked them. They said that you just took Uncle Tim down to the station to answer a few questions and he's still there."

"We have evidence enough to charge him with murder," the Giant said. "I put it up to him. I said if he was willing to stay right there where we wanted him as a material witness, we wouldn't charge him with murder—yet."

"Is that the way you do things in a one-horse place? It's irregular."

"Is it? At any rate, he's safe."

Thompson laughed. "I hope that your beds are comfortable. The old boy likes his sleep. And I guess he couldn't do much to save the missus and the boys if anybody wanted to murder them."

"The police are taking good care of the missus and the boys."

"Police in the doorway, police in the attic and cellar, police in the kitchen and parlor?" Thompson's mocking voice was just a little too casual.

The Giant nodded. "Don't worry about your wife and children. We'll protect them as well as if you were doing it yourself," he said.

Just at that minute, the door opened again and in walked Natalie and Junior. They were wearing matching slacks and sweaters, like twins. And even their expressions looked a little alike.

Natalie came over and kissed me on the cheek. I hate kisses that don't mean anything. "We're getting married," she said. "And we're going to take Donny along with us to be our bridesmaid."

For a furious moment I thought, "No—no—don't get Donny mixed up with your wedding," and then Thompson said:

"Of course. Shall we dress him in pink chiffon with a big brimmed hat and a bouquet of roses and baby's breath?"

Natalie giggled and Junior echoed her with an only slightly less feminine giggle. Donny burst in the door with a puppy in each hand. "Can I, Mom, can I, huh?"

Thompson answered: "Of course, if it's legal. Or isn't that important?"

"Very important," said Natalie. "And while you're lending me your son, you might also lend your husband. Any other loans or gifts welcome. What about some peach-colored tomatoes?"

Junior turned absolutely white for a moment and Thompson was strangely flustered. "Those tomatoes caused a murder," I reminded them all.

EIGHT

"Growing a tomato in sand and water seems like such a silly cause for murder." Natalie's voice was thin and a little shrill and she dabbed at her heavily painted lips with an overlong red fingernail.

"If you put it that way, yes." I remembered enough of Uncle Tim's lectures to explain: "But think of what Uncle Tim's new formula could do to the food supply of starving nations."

"So he murdered the Duchess to keep her from getting a formula. It begins to sound vaguely familiar. The F.B.I. men will be along any minute and some spies are probably hiding in the woodshed."

Donny howled with unexpected laughter. "Just like a serial. Bloody Robertson found a formula and killed four Nazis in the last installment."

Natalie laughed, too, and reached for another cigarette.

"But I'm not joking. It's important." I turned to the Giant. "You know it is important!"

The policeman nodded. "A little farm and a few chemicals can be made to grow some hundreds of times as much as the same small farm could grow under ordinary conditions. That is enough to kill a woman for—or a man."

"But that's magic!" Natalie's thin coy voice sweetened into saccharine approval. "A little window box and a formula can feed a city."

It wasn't that simple, I tried to explain, but they wouldn't listen to me. It captures the imagination, to think of a little seed and a little sand, a few chemicals and a little sunshine, suddenly sprouting tomatoes or potatoes, peas or beans or carrots in bountiful profusion.

It was a yeasty sort of magic—nobody knew it better than I who had listened for so many hours to Uncle Tim talking about the garden cities of tomorrow.

Thompson kept coming back to the wonder of it. He kept talking about all the money that could be made out of the formula, and, listening to him, I suddenly knew that the hydroponic formula had something to do with his return. I got up and walked over to the chair beside him and sat down again, taking a cigarette out of the box on the little side table as an excuse for having changed my place.

I lit the cigarette with vague distaste. I hadn't smoked much, these last years. Under my breath, while Natalie was chattering, I asked my husband: "How long have you been here in town?"

He raised his eyebrows at me. "A little wifely, aren't you, after all this time? What's the matter? Did you miss the fruitcake? You're a great creature of habit, my dear wife. You've been keeping your fruitcake in the same tin box for the last eighteen years. I knew just where to find it. And my key still fits the door. You haven't even changed the lock in eighteen years."

"I haven't changed husbands in eighteen years, either," I told him tartly, "but I'll remedy that as soon as we're out from under all this talk. Thompson, how did the papers get that story about me as the heroine of the occasion? Did you give it to them?"

"Of course. I thought that you'd need a little friendliness from the reporters. Later they may find out a few other things about you—it may help you to have a few friends among the reporters."

The room seemed suddenly overcrowded with people who seemed to press in upon me. The Giant swelled to preposterous height, Natalie's voice grew shriller and Thompson's smile stiffened to a leer.

Had he finally discovered what had happened to me during that lost year?

The terror lengthened and broadened. For the first time I was aware of the sound of words, right there in the room. Natalie had stopped talking, and Junior was saying: "Too bad about Mother, but I'm not going to let her spoil my honeymoon, the way she has spoiled everything else in my life."

The Giant looked at him and then stood up and made his way to the door. "You'll stay in this town where the police department can reach you," he said, "if you don't want to be placed under arrest as a material witness to your mother's death."

Thompson's voice suggested: "A convenient tag, Mr. Policeman. Everybody is a material witness, something a little less than an accessory after the fact and perhaps just a little more than an interested bystander like me."

The Giant looked down on Thompson with emotionless eyes. "I'm by no means certain about your label, Mr. Fenton. Will you come into the next room with me, please, for a little private questioning?"

They went into the dining room and closed the door after them. Uncle Tim had been too careful about sound-proofing and insulation to permit their voices to be heard through closed doors. I could only thank my lucky stars that I had told the Giant about Hugo before Thompson told him what he knew—or thought he knew.

I had botched the whole job of living. It was ridiculous. You'd look at me and see a middle-aged, rather fat woman, moderately good-looking, not too domestic, a creature of routine and habit and maternity. There seemed to be nothing left of a girl who could run away from home to go on the stage, who could live a rather wild life and marry a man still reaping his wild oats. That girl was the kind to whom things happen.

She was always getting mixed up in turmoil. Her very wedding day was a mesh of deceit and murder and flight. She pretended a loss of memory because she did not choose to be asked to explain her immediate past.

She married a man she didn't love just because she wanted security and peace in a little town. She told him nothing, nothing at all, about her secret life. She made no effort to hold him when he wanted to escape her and the life she had made for him.

I caught sight of myself in the mirror above the bookcase and wondered again if this girl could be the same person I saw in my own mirror every day. It felt a little like twins.

And I didn't much like either the girl I had been or the woman I had become. Somehow I had to get away from everybody. With a mumbled excuse, I went out of the door and up the stairs. Donny went outside with the puppies to join Tommy, and Junior and Natalie went on with their plans, right there in my living room. Thompson must have joined them later, but at the time I went upstairs, he was still taking to the Giant in the dining room.

I tried tears, but tears have always seemed very futile to me. If something very slight happens, it isn't worth crying about, and if it's something terrible, the tears don't help a bit.

I tried swearing. The mother of a couple of young sons always has a much stronger vocabulary than she often cares to use in public.

Nothing helped much, so I put on my best suit and the new hat with the veil and took my silk-lined darning basket downstairs and out of the house with me. I picked the best of Uncle Tim's tomatoes and went straight to the place where they were making preparations for the Hydroponic Fair. He might lose his liberty and his good name, but if I could help it, he wasn't going to lose the thing he wanted most—the blue ribbon for the most unusual tomatoes.

I went to see Uncle Tim afterwards and told him what I had done, but he didn't want to talk.

"All I want," he said restlessly, "is to get out of here. I've got things I want to do."

"We're taking care of your plants. You want me to go down to your print shop and tend to things there?"

To my amazement, he flared into sudden horrible anger. "You stay out of that print shop, Flo, and you keep the kids and that no-count husband of yours out of it, too. I want the dust to stay just where it is till I get back."

And I left the jail, without another word from Uncle Tim.

NINE

Uncle Tim won the prize at the Hydroponic Fair with the tomatoes that I entered for him, and when I went to the jail to take him the blue ribbon, I found him still dazed and bewildered.

"Look, Flo," he told me, "you've got to get me out of here somehow before something else happens. I've got to be there to protect you and the children."

He was little and fragile and old and his voice trembled a little. But his sincerity made me think of him suddenly as a man of strength.

"I'll get you out somehow," I promised recklessly. All the way home I kept wondering how it could be done. And then suddenly, the Giant took the decision out of my hands and Uncle Tim was home with us again.

The Giant brought him in on Sunday morning while we sat at the breakfast table. I'd made waffles to cheer myself and the children, and the funny papers and waffles and raspberry jam were littering the dining room.

The Giant brought him in like a boy bringing home an arithmetic paper with a hundred on it after a month of sixties. "I got him, Mrs. Fenton. Now you'll be all right." His voice dwindled into nothingness as he sat there beaming at all of us and began eating waffles and the rest of the

stuff on the table. I gave him fresh hot coffee and grati-
tude, but I saw that Thompson didn't seem at all pleased,
five minutes later, when he came into the dining room and
saw us all there beaming at Uncle Tim and the Giant.

Uncle Tim was the star of the show. He sat there in his
regular place at the table like a small thin god enthroned
among his worshippers. There was something oddly bird-
like, I thought, about the way he kept turning his head
from one side to another, so he wouldn't miss a word that
was being said. He seemed to be listening, always listening.
It occurred to me at that moment that Uncle Tim seemed
always listening for something important that might be
said in his hearing.

That small perky awareness was especially evident when
he picked up his toast and ate it, like a bird pecking at a
crust.

Uncle Tim seemed very important that morning. When
he had finished eating, he went off with Tommy and Donny to see the dogs and the tomatoes, leaving Thompson
and the Giant and me sitting over the breakfast debris.

Thompson's mocking voice said: "You use your own
methods for putting them in jail and pulling them out,
don't you? Small towns ought to patent the method."

The Giant gave him a quick look and solemnly took
another piece of toast that he spread with my best jam. "He
belonged in jail, we thought," he said shortly. "But we've
got a job to do. And you're going to help us, Mr. Fenton."

We were still sitting there at the table, trying not to
think of the questions we wanted to ask one another, when
Mrs. Yates came in the back door without knocking.

"Yoo-hoo, Mrs. Fenton—Flo!" she called, in a trill-
ing ladylike voice she always used when strange men were
around.

She had on a brand-new black sheer dress and some
sheer gunmetal nylon stockings.

Thompson was on his feet and hovered over her while he almost carried her to a chair. He talked consolingly about her late husband while I waited to see why she had come. The facts came out in a minute or two.

"I'm going away, Flo, and I want to leave my canaries and goldfish with you," she said.

"Of course we'll take care of them for you," said Thompson, as if he had lived next door to her all his life. I wondered how he happened to know her. Surely she hadn't been living there when he went away.

"Thompy," she said, smiling at him with that studied smile of sadness that she could put on so easily, "you are so understanding. I knew I could always count on you."

"Always," he murmured, and the Giant's eyes met mine with sudden humor. I don't know why it should have seemed funny. Certainly the facts weren't humorous. "Deserting husband comes home to deserted wife but spends all his kindness on bereaved neighbor."

Maybe if I had cared about Thompson to be jealous— but I don't have much faith in jealousy anyhow. It always seems such a belittling emotion, as if you were so unimportant that you couldn't trust a man to remember you when you were out of sight.

"No thanks," I told her. "Thompson can keep them up in his room if he wants them and he's staying here, but I hate birds in cages and fishes in bowls. I'll take dogs, myself."

"It's just as well," she said with a sigh. "I may not be coming back, anyhow. The house will be so lonesome without my dear departed husband." She pulled a fancy embroidered handkerchief out of her sleeve and settled down to some tears, real or imaginary. I got up and started clearing the table and the Giant helped me while Thompson went on comforting the widow.

"Look, Mrs. Fenton, I don't like to be too personal," said the Giant when we were in the kitchen, with the door closed between us and the tears, "but are your husband and the blonde old friends?"

"Up to this moment I didn't know that they had ever laid eyes on one another," I told him. "But she called him Thompy, and he used his very best blarney on her."

"Look, Mrs. Fenton," said the Giant again, and this time he opened the door a crack, between us and the dining room.

There were no more tears. Instead Thompson and Mrs. Yates were in each other's arms, kissing as if they had waited a long time for that moment.

A little more shaken than I cared to admit, I closed the door carefully and walked straight to the kitchen door. I took my first deep breath when we were walking down the path to the greenhouse garden where the tomato tanks were placed.

Uncle Tim was sitting there, just looking up at his tomatoes, his bird face eager with pride of them.

"Well," he said, "we made it, Flo. The stuff is a success. I'm selling the formula to Magna Foods next week."

I don't know why I felt a little shocked. For some naive reason I had been thinking that Uncle Tim was going to give the formula to the United State government, but I guess that even a man as selfless as Uncle Tim must want enough money for his work to make it worth while to go on to something new.

"We have things to say to you, Mr. Fenton. May we sit down somewhere?"

"There's a little summerhouse, out past the place where we keep the stepladders."

We found the little house. I turned my head away when we passed the tall stepladder, although I had forced myself to look almost every day at the tomatoes that had probably caused the death of the Duchess.

The weather was chilling a little. Fortunately the tomatoes were ripe. Soon it would be too chilly for easy ripening unless Uncle Tim closed off the greenhouses with their glass panels and kept heat around the tomato tanks.

"I want to talk to you. About the first murder, and about your amnesia."

TEN

The secret year couldn't be secret any more. For the last twenty years it had hung over me, threatening, like an atom-bomber ready to drop its load on a defenseless city.

I had no words to fight. All that I could think of was the children. What would become of them? Uncle Tim was old and they were so young. They needed their mother.

"You had amnesia," the Giant said gently.

But I had to tell the truth. "I didn't have amnesia. It was a put-up job. I never lost my memory. There hasn't been a day for all these years that I couldn't have told you what happened. I pretended not to know. I got away with it at the time. Amnesia was new and interesting. People did lose their memories, especially after shock. God knows there was enough shock for me." I stopped and felt myself shuddering, my teeth chattering.

"It was a good story." The policeman sounded impersonal.

"A very good story. But it wasn't true. I made it up as I went along. It was so easy to tell the story—if I had to. One year I was a glamour girl—young and dashing and even, they said, beautiful. I was mixed up in murder. One minute Hugo was alive and then he was dead, and his blood was on my hands." For a quick moment I could almost smell that blood, remembering that night so many years past.

"Then you came home," Uncle Tim said gently. His hand was on mine.

I nodded. "I came home. But I didn't tell anybody. I had used another name. I was Mrs. Hugo Kiphart. But when I came home I was myself again. And I said I couldn't remember—I'd had amnesia. It was so easy that I almost believed it myself."

I turned to Uncle Tim then, as if we were alone. "Will you forgive me?" I asked.

"Of course, my dear. I've known of this for twenty years. Did you think that you could keep a secret from your old Uncle Tim?"

In amazement I looked at him, at the thin face closed on a thousand secrets of his own. At any time in the last twenty years he could have said to me: "Flo, I know about that year." But he hadn't said a word.

"Let me get this straight, Mr. Fenton. You know about the murder of Hugo Kiphart, of your niece's marriage to him, and her flight, of her pretense of amnesia when there was no real amnesia?"

Uncle Tim nodded. "I knew about everything," he said. "I went to New York just a week before Flo came home. I traced her. I found that Flo had suddenly disappeared and Maria Thomassen had taken her place. I saw the pictures of this Maria. I recognized Flo. I even saw her marriage license printed in a New York paper under her stage name. Maybe it was legal and maybe it wasn't. I traced Flo to a little hotel where she had been living and found out from her landlady where she would be living after her marriage. I saw her go into the hotel with her husband. I saw the husband come out and get a cab. Later I saw Flo go out, too."

Incredulously I listened, my face frozen into amazement that all the time Uncle Tim should have known those things. "How did you know Hugo when you saw him go out?" I asked.

"That was easy. The landlady at your old place showed me a snapshot of the two of you that she had taken. She gave it to me." From his old wallet he took a worn little envelope. The photograph he pulled from the envelope was small and dull, but for one moment the laughing eyes of my Hugo came alive for me.

For the first time I realized why I had agreed to marry Thompson. He looked a little like Hugo. Not much. It was just an illusive touch around the eyebrows and the shape of the nose and chin. No two men could have been more different in character, however, and for a moment I felt a futile sharp homesickness for my lost lover.

The Giant took the picture from my hand and looked at it for a moment. "I'll keep this, if you don't mind," he said, and held out his hand for the envelope that had contained the snapshot. "Can you tell me why you kept all of this a secret for so many years, Mr. Fenton? Why didn't you tell your niece that you knew, that you had seen her husband?"

Uncle Tim looked at me with his usual kindly protective smile. "Flo seemed to find some comfort in the amnesia that she pretended. After all her trouble, she deserved to be free from the questioning that was inevitable if anybody knew about that year in New York. Nobody came asking questions. The papers carried stories, but those were New York papers. Our little town, twenty years ago, used local news largely, except for politics and war stuff, when there were wars."

My own private war with life had me by the throat. I looked longingly at the picture as the Giant put it into its envelope and placed that in his billfold. I didn't have even a tiny picture of Hugo.

"What else did you see, after your niece came out of the hotel?" asked the Giant. Uncle Tim shrugged his shoulders.

He said, "I followed my niece. I caught sight of her as she went into the Waldorf. That was the old one, you know, before the new one was built. She sat there, in the old Peacock Alley, not moving from her chair, looking around anxiously. She kept staring at her wristwatch, the one I gave her before she went away, and finally she got up and went out to find another taxi. I followed her to the hotel again. She went in and came out in a minute or two—not more than five minutes, surely—with a suitcase in her hand and a dark coat over her light dress. She went to the station and went into the ladies' room. She came out, wearing a dark dress under her coat. She checked a package in the checkroom and threw away the check, or dropped it. I picked it up. Then I recovered her package and later destroyed it, after opening it just enough to see that it was a blood-stained white dress."

"You saw the bloodstains and yet you destroyed the dress?" The Giant's voice was grim.

Uncle Tim smiled gently at me. "I knew that my little girl couldn't have done anything very wicked in that two or three minutes. She had stumbled into trouble. I could see that. As soon as I got home I destroyed the dress. I got an earlier train, because Flo was so exhausted that somehow she fell asleep in the waiting room and missed the train."

Horribly, I remembered. I hadn't been asleep. I had been sunk in desperate misery, almost paralyzed with grief. Up until that moment I'd had to move quickly—to get away from the hotel, to get rid of the dress, to change my clothes. I didn't remember dropping the check. Somehow the dress never came to my mind again. It eluded my memory the way things do when they are so horrible to remember that your mind closes down against the thought of them.

"You did all this for me, and didn't even tell me." Uncle Tim seemed closer to me than ever before. I took his gentle old hand and lifted it to my cheek. Anything that I could do for him would never make up for the peace he had helped me achieve during all of those years.

Just at that minute, Tommy and Donny joined us with, of all things, a picnic basket packed with everything up to the chocolate cake I'd made at the same time as the one I'd offered Mrs. Yates. "We're going to the lake and forget it all," said Tommy. Uncle Tim smiled.

"I'm going to the office," he said, and walked across the lawn. The Giant followed and they talked earnestly together as they walked.

ELEVEN

We picked our way down the bank to the shore of the lake and settled ourselves and the picnic basket on the grass.

The picnic was a little oasis. For a while I even lost my feeling of panic. "Mom," said Donny, "when I die and go to heaven will I have chocolate cake like this every day?"

I managed to laugh a little. "You will if I'm anywhere around to make it for you, young 'un," I said, and then the Giant came stalking down the grassy shore and the peace and laughter were gone again.

My sigh must have been perfectly audible to him, but he didn't have the grace to look ashamed of himself as he sat down and helped himself to a banana with one hand and a piece of chocolate cake with the other.

"I'm in heaven now," he said. "I expect my wings to come floating down any minute. Look, do you always leave your door open when you go out on picnics? Any murderer could walk in and hide. I brought the key."

Defensively I argued: "But Uncle Tim didn't have his key and it's too much to expect a man his age to climb in the window. I had to leave the door open or the key in the mailbox or under the mat, and I thought that one was about as safe as the other."

Suddenly the pain of all the trouble seemed intolerable to me. I had to get away from everybody. I stood up and walked blindly away from the rest of them. The children were busy with their chocolate cake, but the Giant followed me. "Look," he said, "must you walk in the lake?" He tucked his bandanna handkerchief into my hand and walked me over to a tree stump a few yards away from the children.

"What are you going to do to me?" I asked desperately.

"Nothing, right now. I've timed the whole business with your uncle. He even had a timetable at the print shop and some notes he had written down at the time just in case they would ever be needed. When he saw the New York papers with the news of your first husband's death he knew that you must have found him when you went back to the hotel. According to the timetable and his list, there wouldn't have been time for the murder. I agree with him that somebody got you away from the hotel in order to murder your husband and planted your wedding veil and marriage license to frame you. The letter was planted to give you an apparent motive for murder."

"And for twenty years, I've been living on the edge of a volcano, expecting the police to catch up with me."

"It might have been very unpleasant, very cruel, Mrs. Fenton," the Giant said, "but if you were innocent, the chances are that the police would finally have established your innocence and you'd have been free of all this for the last twenty years."

"Innocent people have been convicted before this. And I had no way of proving that I was innocent. That letter. . . . That blood. . . ." I shuddered at my own memories.

The Giant looked sharply at me. "If you were innocent, I said, Mrs. Fenton. It is still possible that you found the letter and killed your husband, that you came here and established yourself, getting away with your story about amnesia. Then, in some way, the Duchess may have discovered your secret. You may have killed her to keep her from telling. Mr. Yates may have seen something. You may have killed him to prevent him from telling what he saw."

"It seems very logical-—the only thing is that I didn't do any of it. Do you think, Giant—Mr. Antwerp—that I'd risk the security of my children by murder? Those children are more important to me than anything in the world."

"But if you were already a murderer—if this was the only way to keep them from knowing that you were a murderer—" He stopped and I looked at him in horror. "If you had gotten away with it once, you might try again—and again."

"You don't really think so?"

"I don't know. I like you, Mrs. Fenton. If you're innocent you've had a bad deal and you ought to be given every chance to live out your life with your children without the shadow of murder. But if you are guilty, those children would be better off in an orphan asylum than with you, no matter how much you love them."

And with that he went back and sat down beside the boys. He pulled a couple of funny books from his pocket and handed them to Tommy and Donny and sat watching them and me. Without words, I began to pack up the few remains of lunch and then threw myself down on the grass with my eyes closed.

Against my hot dry eyelids, crazy pictures began turning.

Hugo and the letter and blood.

The Duchess on the stepladder.

And then suddenly I remembered about the diamonds, and sat up straight with my eyes wide open. "You asked me about the diamonds, Giant, and I couldn't remember. I remember now. When the Duchess climbed the stepladder she had on the diamonds, that dirty necklace and the two bracelets and three rings that she always talked about. But when I saw her die, the diamonds were gone. I remember now. I kept thinking, the other night, that there was something I must tell you about. It was the diamonds. Somebody stole the diamonds."

"Red herring?" asked the Giant, but I shook my head.

"The truth," I said. "I remember now seeing the sun flash on the diamonds, when the Duchess climbed the stepladder. I remember wondering how diamonds that looked as dirty as Five and Dime rhinestones could flash fire like that when they needed cleaning. And then, later, when she was lying on the ground, dying, the jewelry wasn't there."

"Who took it?"

"The murderer, I guess."

"Look, Mrs. Fenton, it sounds like a joke to say that the woman may have had three murderers. You thought that I was joking when I told you that the step on the ladder was sawed through so she would fall, that she had taken some sort of poison by mouth within five minutes before death, and that she had a knife in her back. All of this suggests an ironical murderer, with some sort of insane feeling of fantasy about this particular victim."

"But couldn't some of this be slanted toward another victim? How would the murderer know that the Duchess would be the next to use the stepladder? How was the poison given? The knife, I'll grant you, probably was intended for her. But the other things—I don't know."

"You used the stepladder usually? Or the boys? Or your uncle?"

"Nobody used it except Uncle Tim. We all had orders to stay away from the tomato tank and the stepladders. The whole greenhouse was his private place, as private as his print shop—and none of us dares to go in there and disturb his papers."

We went on like that for a long time.

TWELVE

I think now that that whole month was a series of escapes and returns. I took the children along whenever I could. I kept thinking: "I'll give them something nice to remember about the life I'm giving them. I'll have to let them know tragedy, but I can give them a little happiness to make the tragedy easier." A little incoherent, but that's how I felt.

We even went to the Zoo. That is how I happened to run into real danger.

The bear was rebellious. It was a big haughty white bear, and some young people were teasing it.

There were two, especially, who seemed to be having a lot of fun tossing things into the cage and even poking their hands in to offer the bear peanuts and then pulling away the nut before the bear could reach it. Bears probably don't like peanuts. The big white bear was disdainful of them, but he didn't like the almost hysterical teasing.

We started to get about as far away from there as possible when I realized that I knew the two who were teasing the bear.

Natalie's shrill laugh and her bright sharp long fingernails infuriated me almost as much as they did the bear, and I thought that the Duchess' son, who was with Natalie, was getting entirely too much pleasure out of baiting the animal.

Natalie saw me before I could get away. She pounced on me.

And from around a corner of the bear's cage came Thompson, my husband. He was wandering through the Zoo with Junior and Natalie. "Some of my best friends are monkeys," he said. "And did you ever meet this bear? He has a heart of ice, even colder than yours, my dear wife."

Natalie laughed: "We saw the note you left for Uncle Tim, saying that you were taking the kids to the Zoo, so we followed you to grab Donny. I've set my heart on having him at my wedding today."

"But I thought that the Giant said you couldn't get away until the case was solved and so you decided to wait."

"Junior wouldn't wait," said my husband. "He's afraid that if he waits too much longer, Natalie will elope with me."

"Not with your wife and the fascinating widow Mrs. Yates sitting on the sidelines." Natalie looked at him strangely for a minute, and then I realized what was happening.

Never for a moment had I figured that Natalie was marrying Junior because she loved him. I even doubted that he loved her. But he did want to be with her and their companionship seemed important to both of them. But now Natalie was falling in love with Thompson.

And Thompson was married to me. That wouldn't last very long. I'd see my lawyer, I thought, the very next time I could go down Main Street. But Mrs. Yates obviously had filed claim on him, too.

I put my hand on Natalie's arm. "Are you sure that you want to be married?" I asked. Natalie's face hardened.

"I'm very certain," she said. She looked at the ring on her hand. There was something familiar about it, although to my undiscerning eye one diamond is pretty much the same as another.

I realized then what was so strange about Natalie today. She was wearing the Duchess' diamonds. Necklace, bracelets, rings, all neatly cleaned but still in their old-fashioned settings. I didn't see how I could have missed them, except, as I have said, that I'm one of those women who cares so little about jewelry that you could palm off the Hope diamond on me for a Five and Ten trinket.

A shiver of fear swept over me as I looked at the diamonds and then at Junior. As I met his eyes I saw in them that same cold menace I had met the night he had threatened me.

So far as he knew, I had not mentioned to the police that I had seen the jewelry on his mother before the murder. So far as he knew, I had not noticed that she was wearing them. Like everybody who knew me, Junior was aware of my indifference to jewelry. Maybe that look wasn't menacing, but only watchful.

"I am getting married today. We have the license and have had all the blood tests made and we're ready to fly off the diving board into the sea of matrimony." Natalie's laugh was even shriller than usual.

Donny and Tommy came wandering up from the monkey cages and I sent them away for ice cream cones and cotton candy. That was how they happened to be gone when the accident happened.

I thought that I heard Donny's laugh over by the monkey cages, and that was how I happened to have my head turned away when the bear seized Natalie.

She and Junior had been teasing that bear for a long time before we got there, and all the time we were talking, Natalie kept poking a stick through the bars of the cage. I had warned her once or twice that it was dangerous, but it didn't do a bit of good. If you are a baiter of bears, no warning ever helps.

Natalie's shrill shriek made me turn so quickly that I almost knocked down a boy scout running past me toward the cage. "He's got her arm. The bear is trying to tear her arm off," he yelled at the top of his voice, and everybody began shrieking and running and pulling all at once. So many people bumped me that I couldn't get near her, although I don't know that I could have helped her anyhow. The boy scout got the bear's keeper and a doctor materialized out of the crowd, and the first thing we knew, we were all sitting in a corner on the grass, shaking with the horror of what had happened. The ambulance had come and gone.

Tommy said: "Somebody pushed her. Somebody pushed her. I know it. Else that bear couldn't have got her arm through the bars of the cage."

Thompson said shakily: "I don't see how anybody could, because nobody was near her except us. We ought to call the hospital soon. They may know . . ."

We were still sitting there, trying to reconstruct the accident, when Uncle Tim turned up. "I got your note and decided to join you. I know you're always somewhere around the monkey cages or the bear pits," he said. "What's wrong? And where are Junior and Natalie? They said they'd be here."

We fell all over ourselves to tell him, and he said: "I must have been just around the corner of the cage when it happened. I wondered why all the excitement. Will she lose her arm?" I nodded, remembering the way the doctor had frowned over it, and we all stood up and gathered things together for our trip home.

THIRTEEN

This time a few simple questions weren't enough. They dragged us off to the police station, all of us, and such questions I hope never to hear again. They talked to us separately and all together. They asked questions and then they asked more questions and then the first ones all over again.

It all came out to the same thing. None of us had seen anything. We had all been within a few feet, even Uncle Tim. Not the boys, thank goodness. They were beyond the monkey house, over at the ice cream bar.

Of course, Natalie's arm had to be amputated. It was so badly mangled that there wasn't a chance of saving it. She wasn't able to tell any story at all, and I changed my mind about Junior's affection for her when I saw him after he came from the hospital.

Thompson was a nervous wreck, too, and the boys took the whole business very hard. It was much worse, somehow, than the deaths of the Duchess and Mr. Yates.

After all, Natalie, in spite of all her faults, was cheerful, and very good company, and she had been planning a marriage with Donny as one of the chief attendants.

I wasn't any too calm myself, especially after the boy scout testified that I was going around pushing people, that I'd pushed him hard enough to push his arm into the cage if he had been close to the bars.

Worse than that, I couldn't remember. Maybe I had pushed her a little, unconsciously, in the crowd. But if she hadn't been teasing the bear by poking things into the cage, her arm wouldn't have been near enough for the bear to seize it and nearly tear it off.

Junior told about the jewelry. They took it from Natalie and gave it to him to put in his safe deposit box for her. It had always been his, he said, left him by his grandmother for his wife, but his mother always wore it. One of the reasons she hadn't wanted him to marry, he told the Giant, was that she'd have to give up the diamonds.

Our supper over, we sat on the porch, talking and looking out across the yard to the dogs' pen where the boys were trying to teach the puppies some tricks.

Thompson was oddly quiet and shaken. I saw him glance, now and then, at the next porch where Mrs. Yates sat rocking, listening to something sentimental on her radio.

She looked very lonely, and very pretty in that half-light.

I hated to bring Thompson back to the present. "Tell me," I said, "what you've been doing all this time, what you've learned, where you've been. Then we can talk about what we're going to do."

"Talk—talk—that's all you ever want to do," he said impatiently. "That's why our marriage would never have lasted, even if I had stayed. I always wanted the future and you wanted the present. Neither of us ever wanted any past. You ran away from yours. I ran away from mine."

"Yes," I acknowledged, "I ran away from mine." I waited for him to tell me what else he knew.

"Your amnesia was a fake and I knew it. I even suspected that you were mixed up in a murder. I saw bloodstains on your white satin slippers and on the nightgown you had packed away, the one you asked me to bring to the hospital the night that Donny was born."

"And you ran away from blood on a slipper and blood on a nightgown."

"Yes."

I understood a little. I had remembered the blood on the wedding dress and I had disposed of it—at least I had checked it and Uncle Tim had destroyed it. But I forgot completely that the white slippers I had worn might have a bloodstain too, and that my white satin wedding nightgown had been lying on the bed not a yard away from Hugo's body and might easily have had a spot of blood on it too. I had packed it away with the rest of my trousseau things and hadn't thought of it again until I needed extra gowns at the hospital when Donny was born. Then I asked Thompson to bring it to me and hadn't thought about it from that moment to this. He hadn't brought the gown. So far as I knew, it was still packed away in that old suitcase up in the attic.

"I want to tell you, Thompson—" I began. "I should have told you before we were married."

But Thompson interrupted me. "Don't tell me anything. Get yourself a divorce tomorrow if you want to, and I'll clear out as soon as the police let me. I'm going next door. I have something to tell Mrs. Yates."

"You know her well, don't you, Thompson?" Uncle Tim's gentle voice broke in.

"Damned well, and she's what I want," Thompson said firmly. "I like Natalie, but I want a girl my own age and with a little more experience than Natalie has. Rosie and I will be married as soon as you divorce me. Want me to move my things next door so you can sue on a desertion or adultery charge and get the divorce sooner?"

He didn't wait for an answer. He strode across the lawn and went up on the next porch and I heard the shrill voice of Mrs. Yates greeting him.

Well, he'd have the kind of wife he wanted, finally, and I'd be free, after eighteen years.

Uncle Tim said: "I shouldn't have urged you to marry him. But I thought that he'd be safe for you. I wanted you to have security after all your trouble, and he looked like security to me. I'd do anything to make things easier for you."

"You're a darling, Uncle Tim. You've done everything for me, already."

Uncle Tim didn't answer. He lay back in the bog chair, looking at the growing shadows, and pretty soon his eyes closed and I heard the even quiet breathing of an old man sleeping.

I tiptoed into the house. Everything was quiet except that a couple of neighbors' children had joined our boys in the yard and Tommy was telling, at the top of his voice, what he was going to do when he was old enough for the Marines.

On impulse I went upstairs. My room was quiet and I thought of lying down on the bed for a nap. I was exhausted after all the questioning and cooking meals and keeping house.

But then I continued up the stairs to the attic.

The door at the foot of the steps were locked, but I had a key on my ring and the key turned easily in the lock.

There was a bulb in an old lamp at the head of the attic stairs.

The air was a little musty, but I opened the window, the one that faced toward the Yates house. I heard Thompson's laugh and Rosie Yates' answering giggle. Well, they'd be happy, anyhow.

I found the old suitcase finally, tucked in a corner under some boxes that I hadn't moved even in housecleaning time.

The nightgown was neatly folded, and I didn't see the brown splotch until I'd unfolded it. I touched the fabric. It was soft except at that one spot, and there it was stiff and brown. It might have been a brown mud stain, or iodine, but it wasn't.

It was Hugo's blood. In that moment, as I stood there in the attic beside the open window with the bloodstained gown in my hand, the feeling of loss that swept over me was almost too much.

And in that moment, with my throat burning with grief I couldn't melt into tears, I was almost killed.

A blind agony of fear made me jump away from the window, but by that time the shot was fired. They asked me later where it came from and I couldn't tell them. All I knew was that at one moment I was standing at the window looking at the blood-spotted gown, and at the next I had stumbled to the floor and the light was out. Afterwards I learned that the shot had broken the bulb. At the time I knew only that I heard the crash of the shot and broken glass and then I was in darkness.

Panic seized me. This was no accident. This was another murder attempt that had miscarried only because I had moved a little to get a better light on the blood spot I was examining. I didn't budge. I couldn't.

I just crouched there on the floor with the smooth cold satin in my hands, my breath coming in a half-sob, half-whimper. My chest hurt as if I had been running for a long time, and I had skinned my knee when I stumbled to the dirty attic floor. I wanted to call out for help, but I had no voice.

How could anybody fire a bullet into an attic window? Within range of fire there were only two things—the attic of Mrs. Yates' house and a tree that the boys sometimes used to play in. Uncle Tim had fixed two ladders and some platforms in such a way that it would have been easy for anybody to climb the tree. And a person standing on the top platform could easily have aimed a gun through that open window at the figure in front of the light—me.

What would I have given for Donny's flashlight at that moment!

Surely there ought to be a flashlight among Tommy's scout things. I stumbled across the attic floor that seemed suddenly overcrowded with obstacles, but there was no need for further search. At that moment the attic stairway door opened and I could see a figure standing in the doorway.

FOURTEEN

Standing there in the doorway was Uncle Tim. He still looked a little dazed in the flare of the flashlight he turned toward his face so I could see who he was. "Are you up there, Flo?" he called. "Did you hear a shot?"

"More than heard it. Somebody shot at me."

"Are you hurt?"

"Only my vanity. I thought I was much too well liked for anybody to try to kill me. My best disposition probably wasn't good enough. Hold that light so I can get down the steps without breaking a leg, will you? Is there danger of fire? The light bulb was shot."

He turned the light on the stairs and clicked the button at the foot of the stairs. "No more danger now." he said. "The light's out and we'll get things cleaned up in the morning. Whatever were you doing up there?"

"Finding something I wanted. Uncle Tim, there was a bloodstain there. On the gown. Hugo's blood. I loved him very much."

Uncle Tim didn't answer. He just sighed a little, hopelessly, as the very old sometimes sigh.

All that night I slept with the foolish white satin gown under my pillow and I dreamed of Hugo, debonair and loving and possessive. But then Thompson and Donny and Uncle Tim came in, all armed with guns, and Tommy tried to take them away to save me. At about that time, while the shooting was going on, I woke up sobbing in my sleep, with my pillow wet with tears.

And in the morning when I answered all questions with a little more casualness than I felt, I was hideously depressed, and more unhappy than I remembered having been for years.

I watched Thompson carefully whenever he came near me all that day. He went next door twice and once I saw him and Rosie Yates up in the attic of the Yates house, going through a big old trunk that had belonged to Mr. Yates. He kissed her, right there at the window, and I thought how easily they could have been shot, both of them, by somebody up in our attic.

Could one or the other of them have shot at me from the Yates attic? But why should either of them want to kill me? I was going to divorce Thompson. They could be married in a few months. And Thompson need never see me again if he didn't want to.

Rosie Yates had no reason for wanting to kill me. I wasn't trying to hold Thompson. There was nothing else.

Unless I knew more than I thought I did about the murders. Unless I had seen something that would convict either Thompson or Rosie Yates of one or both of the murders and I had to be gotten out of the road before I remembered what I knew.

It was too much for me.

I heard Uncle Tim up in our attic and then he went out to the greenhouse. I joined him after a while. "I destroyed those shoes, Flo, but I couldn't find the gown," he said. I started to tell him that I'd taken it down to my room, but just then Thompson and Rosie came over, hand in hand, like a couple of schoolchildren, beaming at each other and then at Uncle Tim and me. Somehow I never got around to telling Uncle Tim about the gown, and he hadn't seen it when I crumpled it into a small ball to take downstairs. That old silk-satin crumpled up into a tiny space. They called it wedding-ring satin, I remembered.

Rosie looked very pretty. There was even a rosy flush in her cheeks, and I don't think that it came from the drugstore. "Wish me better luck than you had with him, Flo. I'm going to marry Thompson as soon as you'll give him a divorce."

I liked her better at that moment than ever before. "I'll see my lawyer today," I promised. "I'll probably need him, anyhow, to keep me out of jail," I added, with a smile to Uncle Tim. Uncle Tim didn't seem amused.

"You won't go to jail," he said. "Not after what I told Antwerp and gave him." I had to think a minute before I remembered that Antwerp was the Giant.

"Any of us can go to jail. It could happen to me," said Thompson, smiling at Rosie.

"Do," she said, "and I'll come visiting with my little basket and hide files and dynamite in the puddings."

"Have you heard how Natalie is this morning?"

Rosie had called the hospital. "Things are pretty bad," she said. "Her arm has been taken off and she may recover or may not. She lost a lot of blood and it seems her heart is none too good."

"Maybe she won't live to wear diamonds," I found myself saying.

Thompson said sharply: "What do you mean by that? Where are the diamonds?"

"So far as I know, Junior has them. They're his. His mother wore them, and then he let Natalie wear them. I think that's why she was marrying him—to get the diamonds." I wondered again how anybody could care so much about ordinary sparkling stones.

Uncle Tim left about that time. "The shop," he said. "I'll be home for supper." He went into the house and came out with a package, neatly wrapped in newspaper.

I called my lawyer and told him about the divorce and he made a few suggestions.

There weren't any rooms in the hotel, so Junior suggested that Thompson move in with him. "The house seems big and empty without Mother," he said. "I'd always looked forward to a celebration when she died, but somehow I miss the old girl. And I'm spending all my spare time at the hospital these days, anyhow. Do you think Natalie will marry me, now, while she's still at the hospital?"

For a moment I really liked Junior—he didn't let himself be scared off by mere physical handicaps. He had learned, in those few hours, that there are things more important than mere perfection of body.

But at that minute, Junior took from his pocket a necklace in a gray velvet case. When he looked at the diamonds his eyes seemed strangely brilliant, as if they reflected the brightness of the stones.

And I wondered again whether he could have killed his mother to gain possession of the diamonds and of his own freedom.

No, we couldn't cross Junior off the list yet.

I went into the room where Thompson was packing. "Are you sure you'd better stay with Junior, Thompson?" I asked uneasily.

He laughed at me. "Don't make noises like a wife," he said. "Even if Junior's a murderer, and he may be, I can take care of myself."

FIFTEEN

I went downtown and signed papers and set things in motion so that Uncle Tim's lawyer, Kleinert, could start that suit for divorce. Thompson seemed eager for it and it didn't bother me one way or another. Desertion was the easiest charge. It was true enough. I didn't suppose that anybody'd raise any rumpus over the nights that Thompson had spent under our roof since he'd come back. We'd been well chaperoned and had had separate rooms.

Uncle Tim didn't get home for supper. At nine o'clock I got a little uneasy and called his print shop. He was angry. "Let me alone, Flo. Surely a man is entitled to a little privacy."

He wasn't alone. I heard somebody talking, there in the shop, and I stopped worrying and went out on the porch and settled myself with a book under the porch light. The boys had three neighbors' children in to help play with the puppies and they'd concocted some sort of new game that threw a spotlight from a flashlight on the puppies while they were doing their new tricks. Fortunately the flash bulb burned out in time so I didn't have to stop their fun, and they all settled down to talk about the scout troop.

I was still sitting on the porch when Thompson and Junior came in. "Natalie's better and I think I need a drink," Junior informed me.

I started to get up, but Thompson said: "You look tired. I'll get it. Do you still keep it on the top shelf next to the fruitcakes?"

Too bad that I was losing a husband, I thought, just when he was starting to be helpful, but Rosie could use him and I didn't really want him.

He came out with drinks and cookies, and we all sat around for a while, nibbling and talking and drinking. The boys had just had cookies and cokes so they didn't have any of ours, but Uncle Tim came in afterwards and decided on a tall drink and a batch of cookies instead of dinner. He had had a sandwich with some people he was seeing on business, he said. We were discussing everything from marriage to murder when all of a sudden Uncle Tim almost doubled up with a sudden pain.

"Appendix," I said, but Uncle Tim shook his head.

"I left my appendix on the cutting room floor years ago. Ouch." His face was contorted with pain. I went in to call the doctor but the line was busy, so I called Tommy and told him to keep trying. Then I went to the medicine chest for an emetic. It sounded as if Uncle Tim had eaten something that disagreed with him. I grabbed the bottle and administered the dose, not knowing whether I was doing; the best thing for him or the worst. But I couldn't stand the look of pain on poor Uncle Tim's face.

"I'm thirsty," he kept saying. "I'm cold." I wrapped him in a blanket and set Thompson scurrying into the house for hot coffee. He brought me some in a cup and some more in a vacuum bottle, and it wasn't until much later that I wondered where he had found the bottle.

The doctor came finally, just when Rosie was having hysterics in Thompson's arms, the boys were trying to tell me how their boy scout leader would have done the job, and Uncle Tim was beginning to feel better.

We got him up to his room and the doctor did what needed to be done. He came down afterwards and said: "I've got to see you alone, Mrs. Fenton." His ruddy face looked worried and his hands were trembling a little with fatigue.

"We'll have to report this to the police, Mrs. Fenton," he said. "It wasn't ptomaine. I think it's arsenic. Tests will be made, of course, but I'm reasonably sure. Was he very thirsty and did he complain of faintness?"

"Yes. But he seemed sick at his stomach, Doctor. He vomited. And then he said his legs hurt, and his skin was very cold. I got some hot water bags on him and gave him hot coffee." I went on to confess about the emetic.

"It was kill or cure," I said. "I was afraid he'd be dead by the time you got here. But we all drank and ate the same things, and nobody else was sick."

"Did he eat supper at home?"

"No. He said he had a sandwich with some friends."

The doctor gave me directions for taking care of him until a nurse could get there. "I can't really spare her," he said, "but you won't need her after tomorrow. I'll have to call her tonight if the Masterson baby starts to arrive, but she'll sleep on the couch in your uncle's room and be there in case she's needed. He'll be all right now. Nice old chap. Glad I could help him. Mrs. Fenton, you'd better not try medication again. You helped your uncle, but you might have killed him if you'd given him the wrong stuff."

Meekly I agreed never to do it again and went back into Uncle Tim's room and closed the door.

The door closed tightly, too. You couldn't hear anything that happened in the rest of the house, which is why I didn't know when Rosie fainted or when Thompson called the doctor back.

The first I knew about Rosie was when I opened the door to see if the nurse had arrived.

She had, and the doctor was there, too. Both of them were in the living room, working over somebody who was lying on the couch. "Donny! Tommy!" I didn't shout, but the words shrieked in my mind as my feet dragged into the room. Just as I got there, the doctor straightened up. "Too late," he said. "She had a fatal dose."

She! It wasn't one of my boys! Then I saw Rosie lying limp on the couch and Thompson slumped down beside it.

Rosie Yates was dead.

This time the Giant came at once. I was in a daze. I got the nurse settled in Uncle Tim's room and then the rest of us got ready for the inevitable questions.

Thompson told, in a monotone loaded with grief, about getting the drinks and the cookies and bringing them out. He told about the coffee and the vacuum bottle. He went on talking and talking and talking but he didn't say anything new.

In my living room some men from the police department were with Rosie, and I thought ruefully that it was too bad she couldn't know how much attention she was getting from so many men. Rosie Yates would have like that.

"We were going to get married. We were going to get out of this one-horse town and get married again," Thompson said.

That brought me up short. "Again?" I asked.

Thompson shrugged his shoulders. "There's no use keeping it secret now," he said. "We met in Alaska years ago. I wasn't working at being married and we lived together for a while. Then she thought she'd like getting married and having a kid, so I said all right. I didn't tell her about you, Flo. After all, Alaska was a long way from home. We got married but the plans about the kids didn't materialize. I was just as well satisfied. I don't like kids much, until they're the age of Tommy, maybe, or Donny."

He was slumped down in a chair now, staring at the un-lighted pipe in his hands. The Giant asked gently: "How long were you together?"

"Five years. Then Yates came along and started spin-ning yarns about what he could give her. I wasn't going to hold her if she didn't want me, so I told her our marriage wasn't any marriage because I had a wife. I told her about you and how I walked out on you, Flo. Then she left with Yates."

The Giant said: "It wasn't coincidence that brought them to this town and landed them next door to this house?"

Thompson shook his head. "That was Rosie's doing. She got Yates to move here. Then she found out that Yates was a four-flusher and she wanted to come back to me. But she didn't have my address, then."

"Where did she get it, finally?"

Thompson shrugged his shoulders. "I don't know. But she got it and she wrote me and I came. I've been in town for a month. I hid out in the room above Rosie's garage until Yates saw me one day, and then I moved to the loft of the old barn. Rosie fed me except when Yates watched too closely. Then I usually raided your kitchen. I still have my key. I just brought your vacuum bottle back tonight. Did you miss it, Flo?"

"But why didn't you show yourself? Why did it all have to be so secret?" I couldn't understand.

Thompson shrugged his shoulders. "It was Rosie's idea of being romantic, and God knows it was little enough to give her along with this old carcass of mine. There are blamed few women who can be romantic at forty-five."

He stopped talking and just sat there, unseeing, while footsteps shuffled past the closed door. Rosie, who had come into my house, so pretty and alive, was going out now, dead.

SIXTEEN

Junior and Thompson didn't stay. The police made no effort to hold them. The doctor left, too, after making some statements and arranging to meet the Giant the next day. When I went back into the living room, everything was as usual, except for some damp newly scrubbed spots on the shaggy wash rug beside the couch and the stain on the table cloth from an upturned cup of coffee. I got the boys up to bed, finally, letting them take a puppy apiece into their rooms to take away the horror of the night, and welcomed the Giant's offer to stay awhile.

The nurse wanted some things to help her settle herself and Uncle Tim for the night, and it was late by the time we sat down to a little peace and some fresh cups of newly made coffee.

The Giant suggested the kitchen, but I wanted to go into the living room. "If I don't go right back now, I'll never want to go into the room again. I'm going in and I'm even going to sit on the couch and have my coffee from the little coffee table where Rosie always put her glass or cup."

The Giant looked at me with approval. "If you'd looked at things that way twenty years ago, you'd have avoided a lot of trouble," he said. "By the way, why don't you tell me the truth now?"

I sat up so suddenly that I almost upset my coffee. "But I did tell you the truth," I protested. "I told you about everything."

"Everything? The shot in the attic? Your uncle fighting with the Duchess? Your husband having a battle royal with Yates the day before Yates was killed?"

"I—I meant to tell you. I was up in the attic, looking at the bloodspot on the nightgown. I was standing at the window with a light behind me and zing-zing—as Donny says—a bullet came. Somebody tried to shoot me."

"Where is the nightgown. Whose blood?"

The wedding nightgown that was in my trousseau when I married Hugo. I never had a chance to wear it. I had it laid out on my bed before I left the hotel room, and when I came back it was still there. There was blood on it and on my shoes. I didn't know it. I put the shoes and gown away and Thompson saw them there, the week he went away. Maybe he thought I was a murderer. I don't know. But he left me. And I swear to you that I didn't see him from the moment he left until the day he walked into my room, just a short time before you saw him. If he fought with Yates I certainly didn't know it. I didn't know he was in town."

"And the diamonds? Junior says that they were in his mother's box all the time. She didn't wear them that day. You told me she did."

"What killed the Duchess? The fall?"

The Giant said that it was the knife. The fall broke a few bones but wouldn't have been fatal. The poison was unimportant. Not a lethal dose. Just a little arsenic, like the stuff that your Uncle Tim and Mrs. Yates had tonight. It may have been a fruit spray. Did your uncle spray his fruit? If she had gotten a tomato with too much spray on it and had eaten it without washing it, that might account for the arsenic."

"But he doesn't use pure arsenic for a spray. Isn't it dangerous?"

"Not if the tomatoes are washed. The spray isn't pure arsenic, of course, but there is arsenic in it. And I think that the coroner will find that the spray with arsenic caused the death of Mrs. Yates and the narrow escape of Mr. Tim Fenton."

We left it at that.

The inquest was routine, just about like the one on the Duchess.

We went to the hospital afterwards, but nobody except Junior could see Natalie. She was just about conscious, still under drugs to deaden the pain, and she only wanted Junior. She asked for Thompson once and he went in and came out with his face white. "It's a damned shame," he said. "That pretty girl—and she'll go through life that way."

"Remember that book about the blind girl? Her mother told her that a physical handicap was easy enough to overcome if you had the character."

"Stop being Pollyanna, Flo. You're a good kid, though. You never liked Natalie, or Rosie either, and yet you've been decent to both of them."

He gave me a look of understanding that startled me. "We might be friends yet, Flo. I like you a lot better than I did when I was married to you. Or am I?"

The lawyer hadn't done much about it and I hadn't had much time to follow him up. "Want me to rush it? I'll do it, Thompson, right away."

But he shook his head. "If you're not in a hurry, neither am I, any more. We'll just go swaggering along as we are. Just forget the divorce unless you want to get married again or something or want to be free."

"We'll see."

We got home late and found Junior on our front porch waiting for Thompson and talking to the boys.

It was while we were talking that Uncle Tim called to us, in his weak old voice. The nurse wasn't there any more. He wasn't sick enough to have a nurse. He was just tired and weak, and he looked very very old. Donny went up to see what he wanted and came back with the idea that Uncle Tim wanted company. All of us were to go upstairs and visit in his room a while.

And it was right there, in Uncle Tim's room, that Junior produced the gray velvet box with the diamond necklace in it. He took it from his pocket and sat staring at it avidly, as I thought I remembered having seen him do once before.

"Give that to me," Uncle Tim said sharply, reaching out his thin, trembling old hand.

Uncle Tim studied the necklace a little. Then he tossed it toward his wastebasket. It fell short, on the bed, and Junior picked it up.

"What do you mean by that?" he demanded furiously.

Uncle Tim laughed a little in a tired old way. "Those aren't diamonds," he said. "As the girl in the story said: 'Is them real rhinestones?'"

Junior turned white and then red. His hands fumbled with the catch of the gray velvet case and he opened it again and took out the necklace.

"Of course it's diamonds. It has always been diamonds. When I had them cleaned, the jeweler said it was a magnificent necklace."

"Who was the jeweler?"

Junior pondered a minute. "I can't remember. Natalie took them in and got them for me. She was the one who told me what the jeweler said."

And that brought the whole business into still more of a turmoil.

"Are the rest of the diamonds like this?" asked Thompson.

Junior shrugged his shoulders in their too well tailored suit. "They're at the bank. Natalie had them all. They gave them back to me and I put them in the bank box, except for this necklace. A bracelet has blood on it, from Natalie's arm. And there's a stone loose in this necklace. I've been carrying it around with me till I get a chance to have it fixed.

"You are sure that you didn't know it wasn't real?" persisted Uncle Tim.

"Do you think," Junior asked in a tantrum of fury, "that I would carry in my pocket and show to my friends a necklace of rhinestones? Do you think that I would give imitation jewels to my affianced wife? Do you think that my Mother would have worn rhinestones?"

He seemed more touched by this discovery than by the death of his mother. As we went down the stairs he kept fingering the gray velvet of the case. And he left, in a few minutes, without another word.

SEVENTEEN

There was a little oasis of peace about that time. Uncle
Tim was getting better. He wasn't able to go down to the
shop much. Twice men came to see him about the tomatoes and he talked alone in his room with the door locked.
Once he became very angry with Donny because he picked
a tomato to take to his teacher and Tommy kidded him by
saying that he was going to have a gold-plated label made
for every tomato.

He came in the kitchen one day, followed by Thompson
who had a basketful of tomatoes. "We want to try canning
them," Uncle Tim said. "We want to test them for keeping
quality, for making tomato sauce and for things like that.
I'd even like to try a little catsup and relish. Not much.
Just a jar each way. There's enough for that."

In dismay I looked at my newly cleaned kitchen and the
flour and things I'd laid out to bake a batch of fresh rolls
for the Women's Club supper. Well, the ladies would just
have to do without their rolls.

Thompson and Uncle Tim sat and watched everything
I did. Thompson helped, more than he ever had when we'd
been married. The kids came in, too, while we were peeling tomatoes. Thompson was much better at sterilizing
jars in boiling water than I. It takes a strong pair of wrists.

By the time we were finished the afternoon was over and we had two of everything. "Like the animals in Noah's Ark," Donny said.

The tomatoes canned perfectly. We did two jars of whole tomatoes, with the skins left on, and two canned whole without the skins. Then there were halves and pulp and a couple of jars of tomato sauce, and two jars of tomato relish and two bottles of catsup. It was a little tricky to fit so many bottles and jars into the canner at once, since they were all of different shapes, but we managed it without breakage. And Uncle Tim packed the jars and bottles in a big carton and asked Tompson to take it up to his room. He didn't even wait until the jars were cold enough to handle easily. He had to have the things up there by night, before the man from Magna Foods came.

It was easier to do everything the way he wanted it than to argue about it, and after a while Thompson came down.

"I left him gloating over them," he said. "He says that the canners never saw tomatoes like that in the history of the world, and I'm not too certain that he isn't right."

I looked at the wreck of my newly cleaned kitchen and wasn't so sure. Two boys and a man can help a lot in an afternoon of canning, but they do make a lot of mess.

Thompson helped me clean up and then amazed me by dragging out the bread things again and announcing that he was going to set some rolls.

"I learned how in Alaska," he said. "This compressed yeast isn't as fine as our own sour dough stuff, but I'll make it do." And he did, and taught me a trick I didn't know. He used double the yeast to the same amount of other ingredients and had his rolls rising twice as fast.

I didn't take the rolls to the supper club meeting. Instead I sat at home with the boys and Thompson and Uncle Tim. "Domestic. Isn't it disgusting?" Thompson

said. "A few years ago an afternoon like this would have
made me desert you. Now I rather like it."

Tommy looked at him. "You know, Pop," he said, "if
everybody except Mom hadn't told me that you were no-
count, I think I'd like you right well."

"A conquest, by Hector. Come to my arms, my noble
son. Have another roll." He tossed one, neatly buttered, to
Tommy, who caught it in his mouth like one of the pups,
and the dinner was finished.

An hour later, Pontifax from Magna Foods came to see
Uncle Tim.

The two men went upstairs to Uncle Tim's room for
consultation and I heard them still talking, three hours
later, long after the boys were in bed, when I said good-
bye to Thompson on the front porch.

Junior came along just when I'd finished saying good-
bye and I had to sit down again while Thompson showed
off his baking by bringing rolls and coffee out to the porch.

Junior said: "I'm going to have something to say to
your Uncle Tim. There's nothing wrong with those diamonds. I talked to the jeweler and he said that they were
as fine as any of their kind in the world."

"Uncle Tim is old and sick," I told him anxiously.
"Please don't start a fight. He's in no condition for any
arguing."

Junior relaxed and took another roll. He even spread it
with a little plum jam that Thompson had put on the tray.
"Well, maybe he hasn't got much sense about anything but
printing and tomatoes," he said. "After all, I can't expect
everybody to be the expert on diamonds that I am."

This was the first time I'd ever heard that Junior was
an expert on the subject of anything but Junior, but I said
nothing. Thompson just looked at me and offered another
roll. "Guaranteed to make you plump and pretty," he said.

"Darned if I don't like that plumpness, Flo. Why didn't I have sense enough to stay home where I belonged?"

"You did better in Alaska," I said dryly. But I took the roll and more coffee, knowing that if I had been different, more loving and more understanding, Thompson would probably never have gone away in the first place.

Just about that time, Junior finished his rolls and coffee, wiped the plum jam from his pretty lips on one of my best linen napkins, and got up to leave. "I guess I won't fight with your Uncle Tim after all. I owe you something, Flo, for making friends with me again after I threatened to strangle you and wanted to rob your house."

Thompson was on his feet in a moment and standing over Junior, jerking him to his unsteady feet by a hand at his collar.

By the time I got Thompson smoothed down by explaining Junior's desperation that night, I had almost talked myself into believing that Junior's actions were justified. The two men were still mumbling at each other when Uncle Tim and his guest came down the stairs.

"Well, Mrs. Fenton," said Mr. Pontifax smugly, "I think that we're getting something big."

"It will revolutionize the industry, I believe the phrase is," Thompson suggested helpfully. Uncle Tim glared at him, but seemed too happy for more than momentary anger.

"Exactly. May I congratulate you, Mrs. Fenton, on your canning? The tomatoes are beautiful. And those allergy tests are coming along beautifully, too."

Junior had withdrawn into the shadows, but now unexpectedly, Uncle Tim called to him. "Junior, this man knew your mother. Mr. Pontifax, this is young Kelcey Stratton."

Junior's reaction was like something out of a slapstick comedy. He took one look at the man and the man took two looks at him. Then Junior set out down the steps and the garden path as fast as his feet would carry him, with the stout sturdy figure of Mr. Pontifax of Magna Foods lickety split behind him. He almost caught up with him, too, but Junior slammed the gate on him, and by the time the older man had it open and started down the street after Junior, there was a wider gap between them.

The last we saw of the two men, they were rounding the corner into Main Street, with Junior about two yards ahead of Pontifax, who was shouting at him something we couldn't understand.

EIGHTEEN

Uncle Tim stood there on the porch, chuckling. Nothing had amused him for a long time as much as this slapstick.

He went upstairs again, still chuckling, locked his door as he had been doing for some time now, and settled down for the night.

Thompson sat down on the steps. "Shades of Mack Sennett," he said. "I expected to see Junior turn and hurl a custard pie in the other guy's face in a minute or two. Of course they'll come around the corner and hurdle a few fences and get splashed with mud before they threw tomatoes at each other."

Thompson didn't go at once to Junior's where he had been sleeping. Instead he just sat there on the porch, yawning now and then, and staring up at the stars.

"They are the same stars here, I guess," he said, "but they look so different in different places. Ever see them in the North? And out in the Southwest on the desert they could be bigger stars brightly minted."

I was curious about Junior but I was sleepy, too. "Tell you what, Flo," suggested Thompson. "I'll lock up for you and stick around for a few minutes until I make sure that our visitors are gone for the night. Then I'll go on up to Junior's for the night and tell you in the morning what happened."

I was willing. I latched the door on the inside, after Thompson had locked up. He had his old key that still worked. I caught sight of him through the glass of the front door, and he grinned and blew a kiss at me, and I went upstairs strangely flustered.

But in the morning Thompson didn't show up. And Uncle Tim left very early before the boys and I were awake. He called about ten from the print shop and said: "I have some business out of town. I'm all right, now; don't fuss about me. I'll be back tomorrow."

I knew that he kept fresh shirts and a razor at the office for times when he had to go calling on the trade after messing around with inks and type all day. But he wasn't really well enough to go wandering around the country alone.

Tommy came up about that time with a suggestion that when he was seventeen he was going into the Marines, and I found myself saying, as women usually did, "Talk it over with your father."

Tommy came back in a few minutes with more questions. "Mom, why do you and Pop have to go and get divorced? He's a right guy. I wouldn't mind having him around the place. He can pitch a keen game of baseball."

I managed to drag a red herring in the shape of a chocolate cake in front of Tommy, but I kept thinking of Thompson most of the day.

Why didn't he go back where he came from? Rosie wasn't waiting for him any more.

That night I dreamed of Thompson chasing me. Only then, suddenly, he turned into Hugo who threw a custard pie at me. I woke up laughing, and was in a terrifically good humor when I went down to fix breakfast. I was losing track of the days.

That day was Saturday, I think, because the boys were home from school. I kept expecting both Thompson and

Uncle Tim, and when neither of them turned up I didn't
know what to make of it. But it wasn't until evening that
I had sense enough to be frightened. I called Junior's
house and nobody answered. I saw somebody up in the
attic of the supposedly empty Yates house and thought
that Thompson might be there. But when I called, nobody
answered there either.

Some time after an uneasily hasty supper I left the boys
playing with some neighbor children on the porch and
telephoned the Giant. He was on the job at that hour, I
knew.

"No. Nothing much has happened. We've been working
on two other cases," he said. "Have you heard that your
doctor found a woman poisoned to death when he went to
answer a call? Her husband did it and lit out, but we got
him before he went over the county line." He was proud
of the accomplishment but brought himself back to my
problems.

"Look," he said, "how about me coming over there? It's
hard to talk over the telephone."

The boys had relinquished the dogs and the porch in
favor of a baseball game out beyond the kitchen garden
when the Giant came striding up the walk, like another
giant in seven league boots.

"Thompson and Uncle Tim are gone off somewhere," I
told him, feeling silly at being worried. I went on to explain when I had seen them last.

"Your husband left all at once like, that once before,
didn't he?" The policeman reminded me. "He's all right. I
have a way of knowing."

I nodded. "But that was years ago. He's different now."

"Men don't change. Their women just think they do.
He said he was going to marry Mrs. Yates. Mrs. Yates died
and you are divorcing him, I think you said, so he's lit out
again. Nothing to hold him."

"But Uncle Tim— And you might tell me why you know about Thompson."

"He said he was going on business and would be back in a couple of days, didn't he? Well, his time isn't up. He's older than Donny and Tommy."

"But I saw somebody in the Yates house and it wasn't Thompson. I thought it might be. I called him but he didn't answer."

I stopped, feeling very silly. But now the Giant was sitting up straight. "Now you're talking. That sounds like something," he said. He went to the telephone and gave a couple of orders.

Tommy and Donny came back and settled themselves beside us.

The boys were eager. "I've got my flashlight," Donny said. "I got a new bulb and some new batteries, the last they had. How about me going with you?"

"I can shoot!" Tommy offered. "I shot Franco's mustache off twice at the country fair last month, and I put a bull's-eye right in the middle of the target."

"You'll make a couple of good Marines in a few years," the Giant said, "but now we just need some common ordinary cops, grown up ones."

He left when Bradfield and the uniformed cop came. I had Rosie's key, the one she had left with Thompson so he could tend to the goldfish and the canaries the day she went to town. I didn't know about it until I found the keys lying with Thompson's notebook on the hall table. "Rosie's key," said the neat label. "Remember to feed goldfish and canaries." That was Rosie. I remembered the time she sent me the pan of shortcakes. "Shortcakes," read the neat label. "Use with strawberries or cherries."

I felt a lump in my throat at the memory of the woman who had been, in a sense, my rival without my knowledge.

She wasn't at all the kind of person I liked. But she was neater than I'd ever be, in her house, her mind and her loves. She knew what she wanted and she set out to get it. She followed recipes exactly, just as she made plans for living and followed them. She made lists and labels and she stuck to them. I always envied that, even if I couldn't see myself doing it her way. But death was one thing that came without a plan for poor Rosie.

Before I got too maudlin I went on in to see if I could call Junior and Uncle Tim again. This time Uncle Tim answered. He sounded excited. "I'm all right, Flo. Don't worry about me. I'm going away again. Don't worry if you don't see me for a week."

Junior was at home. "Natalie's better," he said. "We're getting married this afternoon at the hospital. Can you and Thompson come, and the kids? The doctor says she's well enough today."

I said that the kids and I would be there, at three, but that Thompson had gone away and I didn't know where he was. "Well, bring him around if he comes. Remember. Three o'clock."

Just about that time I heard the Giant calling from the porch of the Yates house. I went out to the door. "Where was that guy? Up in the attic, maybe?"

"Yes. That's where I saw him."

"Somebody's been there. Somebody's been sleeping and eating there. The darned fool even had the canary cage and the goldfish bowl up there for company."

"Not Thompson?"

"Why should it be Thompson?"

"Well, he hid out once before, and he liked Rosie and wanted to take care of her goldfish and canaries."

"No. Not Thompson. I had a note from Thompson yesterday. He's in New York, on business. I wasn't going to tell you, but I'd better."

I felt a sudden surge of relief. Tommy grabbed at my arm. "Pop all right? He's not in jail, is he, Mom?"

I laughed a little, shakily, and shook my head.

The uniformed cop and Bradfield clumped down the stairs to the porch. "Nobody in the house," they said. "We've looked high and low."

"But don't worry, Mrs. Fenton. It isn't your husband. He's in New York, and a man can't be two places at the same time. He's staying at the Prairie Fire Hotel."

NINETEEN

At the name of the hotel where Thompson was staying, I felt a wave of faintness sweep over me. For years I hadn't thought of the name of that little obscure hotel established by some homesick dweller from the prairies. That was the hotel where Hugo had been killed, the hotel from which I had fled on that terrible day twenty years before.

"You see, Mrs. Fenton," the policeman said gently, "your husband is on his way north, but he says he's stopping off to settle some scores. He says to say good-bye to you and the boys. I wasn't going to say anything to you yet."

I managed a smile. But the Giant was very serious. "I've phoned the New York police department to keep an eye on him," he told me. "I have a friend there. If he tries to leave, they'll clamp down on him and phone me and I'll send Bradfield down to get him."

"But isn't he free to go?"

The Giant shook his head. "There is too much murder here, Mrs. Fenton. Your husband may have had his reasons for hating the Duchess and may have killed her. He may have decided that he didn't want Mrs. Yates any more, so he may have killed her. He may have shot at you. He may even have had something to do with the death of your first husband."

"But I didn't—I wasn't married to him then."

"You weren't married to Fenton. But you had dates with him before you went away. Then he went to see you and found you had married another man."

"But that doesn't mean he murdered him. There was the letter and the marriage license and the veil. That looked like a woman's murder."

"The letter may have been in the room. Or Thompson Fenton may have found the woman who hated you because of her love for Hugo. He may have teamed up with her. Did you ever see the real Maria Thomassen or whatever her name was? Or even her picture?"

"No."

"Then she may have been somebody right here in town. She may have come here instead of to South America. She may even have gone to Alaska."

The words sang their way into my panic. I held tightly to the remnants of my sanity. "You aren't suggesting that Thompson and Rosie may have killed Hugo? I don't be-lieve it."

"Neither do I, quite," agreed the Giant. "If I had been sure, if there had been any real evidence, I'd have nailed Thompson yesterday."

"Then who could it be? Junior? There simply isn't any-body else."

"There's you. I could make a good case against you, I think. You may have murdered your first husband. You came home and found him with a woman or the love letter and you murdered him."

"I had no gun. Where did I get the gun?"

"There was no gun. He was killed with a small knife, a small sharp knife that was lying under his body. That knife is still where it can be reached."

"But my fingerprints are nowhere near it. I never saw it."

"There are no fingerprints on the knife. But your fingerprints, Mrs. Fenton, were all over the room. In blood, some of them."

The Giant seemed to bob up and down before me. I was dazed as from a heavy fall. "I couldn't have killed him. I loved him."

"Women have killed the man they love," he said solemnly.

I tried to keep my voice steady. "I'll go back if I must and stand trial. Uncle Tim will take care of my children. But I didn't kill him. I couldn't have hurt him any more than I could hurt Donny or Tommy or Uncle Tim. Any more than I could reach out my hand and kill Donny's pet puppy out there."

"I want to believe you, Mrs. Fenton. To continue, you could have killed the Duchess because she had discovered, after many years, the other murder. You could have killed the Yates, Mr. Yates because he saw you, Mrs. Yates because you were afraid that he might have told his wife. Mrs. Yates died of poison, arsenic, in her drink. There was arsenic in your uncle's drink, too, just enough to make him a little sick and divert suspicion from you. You'd think that I'd never suspect you of hurting the uncle you love."

"This is crazy—you must know that I couldn't be like that. Look at me, Giant—Mr. G. I. Antwerp. I'm a middle-aged woman, perfectly happy with my uncle and children. How could I change suddenly into a murderess?"

We weren't much further along than that when Thompson came home.

He looked tired and was carrying a worn leather satchel. He even had a hat on. Now that I think of it, it was the first time I'd seen him in a hat for twenty years.

"Can I stay here tonight, Flo?" he asked. "Junior's getting married and I thought I'd clear out and give him a chance for a honeymoon."

"But surely Natalie can't leave the hospital yet."

"No. But he wants to get the place all fixed up. The painters and paper hangers move in and I move out."

"Take your bag upstairs," I said.

The boys went with him to help him get settled and the Giant asked: "Afraid? I think I'll move in too until your uncle gets back. My place is being papered and painted, too, and the hotel hasn't any room."

He was lying, beyond a doubt, but I was grateful. A policeman in the house would be a godsend.

He called to Thompson: "Care to share that room with me? Or is there another spare room? I have a deluge of painters and paper hangers in my place too."

If Thompson knew it was a lie he didn't show it. With at least a show of cordiality, he said: "Come on in. I can recommend my wife's cooking. Your testimony will be handy next week, anyhow, if Flo decides she wants a divorce."

We left it at that. I remembered the wedding. "Get out your best bibs and tuckers, everybody," I called. "We're all going to the hospital at three to help Junior and Rosalie get married."

The Giant left, then, but said he'd be back soon.

TWENTY

The Giant's car came driving up just as two men strode up the walk. Reporters. One from the local weekly. The other was a stranger, probably from out of town.

I'd been consistently refusing to answer questions but I knew that Thompson had talked to the reporters several times. This time he came down the stairs and Brant, from the *Weekly Clarion,* hailed him.

"Hi yah, guys," he said. "Heard about the wedding?"

I listened while Thompson told about Junior, about Natalie's improvement, about the way the decorators were being turned loose on the Stratton house, about the family diamonds that Junior was giving Natalie for a wedding present. The reporters loved it—and him.

Finally he said: "Got another bit of news for you, boys." He came over to where I was standing and put his arm around me. "The wife and I aren't ex-ing any more. We've decided to stick it out together from this time on. No divorce."

I started to deny the story, but Thompson's hand around my waist gave me a good strong pinch.

When the reporters had gone and were buttonholing the Giant on the sidewalk as he got out of his car, I asked: "Why did you do that?"

He grinned at me shamelessly. "Never drop one husband till you get another. Stick with me, pal. I'll explain later."

And that was all he said. I couldn't make him talk about where he'd been. I couldn't do anything except get dressed for the wedding and make certain that Donny and Tommy were clean behind the ears and had the cowlicks in their hair smoothed down.

Uncle Tim phoned again, when we were almost ready to leave. I told him about the wedding and he said he'd get there if he could but it wasn't likely because he was leaving so soon. "Remember," he said, "don't put out a police dragnet for me, whatever that is, if I don't get back in a week or two. I'm working with big business."

"But are you strong enough, Uncle Tim?"

"When you're my age you're living on borrowed time anyhow, and that's one thing you don't have to pay back when you borrow it." He chuckled and the telephone line closed.

I went back to the family, standing on the front porch waiting, and we went down the street, "like an average American family," as Donny said gleefully. The two boys walked on ahead, much more sedately and importantly than usual, and finally I got a chance to mention the name of the hotel.

"You did go there, Thompson? The Giant said you wrote him—"

"Yes. Nothing to worry about. I just had to compare a few fingerprints."

"But twenty-year-old fingerprints wouldn't still be in a hotel. And whose fingerprints—mine?"

"Wives shouldn't ask questions. It's a beautiful day for a wedding. I always have sunshine for my weddings. The last two times I was married the sun was shining."

"I remember one time, Thompson."

"A bride cold and frightened, shivering and panicky. You were a pretty girl, Flo, and very sweet. And I almost walked out on you before the wedding."

I stood still for a minute and then walked on slowly beside him.

"Any particular reason?"

"The best reason of all, Flo. I loved you like hell and all you had to give me was a mild casual liking. I stood it for those century-long years. You had all your emotions frozen. You said it was amnesia, but I know now it was shock. I thought that having the babies you wanted might wake you up. But the way you looked at me the night Donny was born showed me what I was losing, and I walked out."

"How did I look at you?"

"Well, for a second you were only half conscious. Then you thought I was somebody else. You looked at me with your eyes alive for the first time in all those years. And you called me Hugo. Then I went home to wrestle with a few of my devils and look for the gown you wanted. I saw the bloodstains and a note to Hugo that you had never mailed. I knew then what was wrong, and I got out as soon as I could."

"It must have been hell, Thompson." I was so shaky I could hardly walk. Thompson took my arm. Ahead of us the boys were walking quietly toward the hospital. Once an acquaintance spoke to me a little curiously, watching Thompson, not me.

"I tore up that letter, Flo. I tore it into scraps and burned the scraps. I felt I was burning up every tie that bound me to this place. I guess I was wrong. You're alive now, Flo. More alive than poor Rosie ever was."

"That's because I've had some years of peace—and the boys and Uncle Tim have been wonderful."

"While I deserted you when you needed me because I couldn't have first place in your life."

"Don't be so hurt, Thompson. It's over now—years ago."

"The life I've led—" He stopped. We were coming to the hospital. We went in, all in a group, and found Junior waiting in the hall. He was talking to the doctor.

"Hello, Mrs. Fenton. I haven't seen you since your uncle has been well. Is he quite recovered?"

"Well enough to run around the country on business."

Junior broke in then, after talking to a pretty nurse. "Natalie's ready now," he said.

We all went up in the elevator, frightened by hospital noises and silences into an unaccustomed quiet. Natalie was in a private room that was bowered with flowers like a county fair garden exhibit.

The pink silk cover on the bed and the filmy white thing she wore hid her arms so I couldn't see the bandages. She had been made more beautiful than ever before, I thought, by luxury and by pain. All the hardness was gone. The pain had given her a quality of fragility that made her more lovely than I had ever thought she could be.

"Hello, bridesmaid," she greeted Donny. "How about a kiss for the bride?" He kissed her, blushing to the ears, and then the minister, Mr. Philips, came in and opened his book and stood talking for a moment while we found our places. Junior was standing beside the bed.

Thompson grinned at him. "Hope it takes, kid," he said. "Marriage isn't such a bad idea, after all. If it lasts next five years it should last a lifetime."

Junior's face looked furious for a minute. "How do you know?" he asked. "You had two women—three—and you couldn't hold any of 'em. You're not an expert."

For a second I thought that Thompson was going to punch Junior's nose. Then he seemed suddenly to remember where he was. He looked at Natalie and their eyes met as if there were some secret understanding between them.

I remembered seeing Natalie stare at him with that look—and more—at the Zoo, just before she was hurt.

Then Thompson grew suddenly white, as if he were going to faint, and I moved closer to him. He said nothing and his color gradually came back. What did Junior know that I didn't? What knowledge, what emotions did Natalie and Thompson share? If Natalie loved Thompson, why did she want to marry Junior? Why had she wanted only Junior when she was so sick, if it was Thompson she loved?

While we stood there, all thoroughly bewildered, Junior took a velvet case out of his pocket—the same velvet case that Uncle Tim had tried to toss into his wastebasket.

Junior opened the box and looked at the necklace. Then he placed the box on Natalie's bed, right where she could look closely at it from where she sat propped up against her pillows.

"Diamonds for the bride," he said. "Many happy returns of the day, Natalie."

Natalie smiled and then avidly looked down at the necklace. Her smile abruptly faded into panic. Then she sat up almost straight, so I could see the pathetic emptiness of one chiffon sleeve. "Is this what you think of me?" she asked.

"Diamonds aren't good enough for you?" asked Junior furiously.

Natalie glared at him. "But these aren't diamonds," she said. "These are imitations. Where are the diamonds, Junior? I wore them once. I know."

Junior was working himself into a tantrum. I expected him to stamp his feet on the floor in a minute and cry like a spoiled baby. "They're diamonds," he screamed.

"Imitations," Natalie countered. "Imitation diamonds for an imitation marriage. I won't marry you, Junior. Go home, all of you."

TWENTY-ONE

The doctor got us all out of the hospital before Natalie's hysterics had risen to a climax.

We adjourned to Junior's house and sat down among all the debris of the decorators. The paper hanger had been steaming paper off the wall; all the furniture was standing in the halls or in the middle of the living room shrouded with tarpaulins.

There was a long table on a pair of horses standing in the middle of the living room. No. It was a parlor. The Duchess had always called it, "my parlor."

Junior perched himself on the pseudo-tables with total disregard for his well-tailored wedding finery. He took the flower from his buttonhole and tossed it to the floor, where it nestled among the shreds of paper steamed from the walls.

"Well," he said, "that tears it. Muffle the wedding bells. Dig out the funeral vaults. Good-bye forever and all that." He lit a cigarette and I noticed that his hand was shaking. Then, with a laugh, he added, "Of course she's all wrong. The diamonds are real. She just doesn't want me, and I don't see any reason why she should, at that."

"May I see the diamonds?" asked Thompson.

Junior shrugged his shoulders. Then he took the velvet case from his pocket and tossed it to Thompson.

The diamonds looked all right to me. But then, how would I know? But Thompson looked puzzled "There's nothing on earth wrong with these stones that I can see," he said. "I'm not an expert, but they look all right."

"They were good enough for my mother," said Junior. "They were good enough for my grandmother. But they're not good enough for Natalie."

"Are you sure that these were the diamonds that she saw? And does she know a real diamond from a fake?"

"Gee," said Donny uneasily, "do we have to stay here? Those puppies are all alone except for their mama. And if something happened, like a fire or a flood or an earthquake or something, she couldn't carry all of them away at once. Can't we go home, Mom?"

"Tell you what, Mom," suggested Tommy. "Donny and me'll go home and fix a wedding feed for the gang. You got that cake you made yesterday and we can open some peaches and make coffee for you and chocolate milk for us and there might be enough baked ham for sandwiches if I stop on the way home and get bread. And I can pick enough stuff for a salad out of the garden and make it the way you let me do the day my gang came to supper. I'm going to be a mess sergeant, so I'm learning to cook in the scouts," he added, to Thompson.

"Wonderful," Thompson said. "The rest of us will be along by the time everything's ready. You'd better do a good job or I'll hang you from the yardarm."

Junior sat there on the table, saying nothing, as the boys went out of the door and down the street. Then Junior turned to Thompson and said with a particularly repulsive smile on his face: "Well, Fenton, don't you think it's about time we had a showdown?"

"I don't get it," Thompson said. "About what?"

"About Natalie. She wanted me and my house and my diamonds. And then you came along and without half trying you got her to turn me down."

Thompson didn't look at me. He laughed a little, uneasily. "Surely, old fellow," he said, "you're mistaken. I
haven't any influence with Natalie. She's just overtired
and hysterical. The doctor should have asked you to wait
a while. That girl isn't ready for anything as exciting as
marrying you, Junior."

Unaccountably the remark seemed to soothe instead
of infuriating him. Junior seemed to be acquiring all of
his mother's irritating pompousness without the dignity
that had helped her neighbors to endure the Duchess even
while they were hating her.

Thompson tossed the velvet case to Junior, who caught
it with unexpected skill. "Stop being careless with more
thousands of dollars than you will ever see again, Fenton,"
ordered Junior, and there was venom in his eyes and mal-
ice in his thin effeminate voice.

Thompson stood up. "I'm sorry that your wedding plans
were changed, Junior," he said gently. "I'm sympathetic
and all that. But if you want me to sit and dry your tears
for the next three hours, you'll have to bait your hook
with something better. Come along, Flo. Junior, your wedding feast is waiting if you care to join us, clad in a little
good humor for a change." He strode to the door and I
followed him. We left the door open and Junior stood in
the doorway watching us all the way down the street.

When we finally got to the corner, he called: "Wait a
minute. I'm coming with you."

And come he did, an angelic smile on his face, an un-
troubled brow above serene eyes. "I don't see how he does
it for the money," I whispered to Thompson when we started up the walk to our house.

And Junior was like that for the next hour at least. He
was gay. He was sprightly. He might have been a bride-
groom toasting his own wedding. He praised the boys for
their excellent cookery. He swore that there never had
been so masterly a salad, that the sandwiches Donny made

were equal to any he had ever eaten. He admired the cake
and relished the peaches. He was hail fellow well met and
adoring friend and sympathetic companion, and by the
time he left we were all so bewildered that exhaustion
almost overcame us when the door closed behind him.

Thompson was the first to laugh and Tommy followed
him with a younger echo of the same note of laughter.
Donny and I joined in until I had to wipe the tears from
my eyes.

Finally Thompson said: "He almost had me thinking
that everything that happened was a mirage. Everything
was all sweetly hunky-dory. Nobody ever was murdered.
Both of Natalie's arms are well, and the diamond necklace
is perfectly too-too sweet."

"That man," said Tommy thoughtfully, "is dangerous.
I know."

"Out of your vast experience, my son," Thompson suggested, "will you please tell us why the man is dangerous?"

"Well, it's like Bloody Robertson figured out in a serial
a couple of months ago. You needn't be afraid of the tough
guys because you know they are tough and you're careful
not to clash. But a guy like Junior—well, he's so silly and
so harmless that you don't worry about him. And he's the
guy who's dangerous because you never suspect him."

"Son, on that broad and noble statement I hereby with-
draw any objection to the hours you spend with Bloody
Robertson. You have taught me things that the world has
been unable to teach me. Now shoo, kids. Your mom and
I are cleaning up the kitchen and some dialogue and we
need the place to ourselves."

They went, too. Tommy made some sort of high sign to
Thompson as he left and Donny raised both hands above
his head and said aloud: "Hi, Champ."

Then I saw them hailing a couple of boys across the
street and turned back to the dishes. But Thompson was

beginning to settle things, too. He was gathering up dishes and piling them as efficiently as I could have done it myself. I put the things in the icebox while he started washing dishes and I dried them. We kept up an inconsequential chatter that meant nothing at all. Finally, when we were finished, Thompson led the way into the living room and deliberately sat himself down on the couch where Rosie had died.

He continued chatting about the tomatoes and the things we had canned and the way Junior had handled the diamonds. Then he stopped and just sat there for a moment, looking at me silently, until I said:

"You might as well say it, Thompson. You've been saying one thing and thinking another for hours. I think it's time to talk now, don't you?"

He nodded and lit another cigarette. "O. K., Flo. You asked for it. You weren't married to Hugo. That marriage was a fake. He was already married to the woman who wrote that letter, that Maria person."

Waves of nausea swept over me. He said gently: "It gives you a motive for murder. And the Duchess is Maria's sister. She knew everything about you and the murder. And she said that you were in the hotel for half an hour, when you came back. She told Junior. And Junior told me. I went to see whether I could rake up anything from an old hotel clerk who has been at the hotel for thirty years. That's how I got a line on him. Some snazzy reporter had a feature the other day. This old hotel clerk told all the tales of things that went on in the long long ago."

"Like murder," I said. My mind was numb.

"Like murder. And weddings. And beautiful brides dressed in white chiffon but with dark coats thrown on hastily over bloodstained white draperies. Bloodstained slippers that left a print on a newspaper on the floor of the lobby, a little white vanity case with a bloody fingerprint on it. All those things were in the news story I saw. That fingerprint got me—that and the footprint in blood."

"The footprint I understand. But I didn't carry any little white vanity case. I didn't own one. I never did like little purses or vanities."

"And that," said Thompson with satisfaction, "is where they made their big mistake."

"Because I didn't own a little white vanity case?"

"Because you didn't own a little white vanity case. Because that fingerprint in blood cannot be yours. And because somehow, we're going to manage to beat the rap."

TWENTY-TWO

As I fell asleep that night there was comfort in knowing that there was a policeman in the house. I dreamed that I was telling Donny to ask a policeman if he got lost and Donny was answering, with terribly real finality in his voice: "But I'm not lost, Mom. You are, and Pop is. Even Uncle Tim and Junior are. But not me."

I was thinking of the dream the next morning when I settled down to my coffee. I'd made puffy omelets with strawberry jam and little biscuits, and the boys and their father and the Giant were engulfing huge amounts of all of them. I kept worrying about Uncle Tim.

The Giant said something about him, too. "I think we'll see what we can do about finding your uncle," he said. "I'm a little uneasy about him. That Pontifax—"

"Pontifax? The man from Magna Foods?" I recalled that unexplained chase with Junior.

"Pontifax isn't from Magna Foods. He's some sort of European agent. We can't be sure about his antecedents, but the F.B.I. has its eyes on him."

"Did you tell Uncle Tim? He's so old and so helpless."

"Yes. I told him but he wouldn't believe me. He's threatening me with a suit for false arrest because I delayed his business by keeping him in the station. But it was an honest mistake, Mrs. Fenton. And I didn't really arrest him, not exactly."

"And when you discovered he was innocent," I acknowledged, "you let him go at once."

"Yes. Now look, all you. I've got some things to say. You kids run out, please, if you've finished your breakfast. We're going to talk about murder. It's no case for kids."

The boys' hungry eyes turned to the biscuits and strawberry jam. You could see that the Giant had no boys of his own.

Helplessly they turned to their father. He went to bat for them. "Giant," he said, "these boys are experts. They know almost as much as Bloody Robertson—or Robinson, I can't remember which. They listen to the best that Radio City and Gangbusters and Counterspy have to offer on the airwaves. Then, when real excitement comes, along with omelet, strawberry jam and biscuits, an unfeeling policeman sends them away. Do I state the case correctly, gentlemen at the bar?" He grinned at the boys. The Giant relented.

"Well," he consented grudgingly, "you can listen. But not a word out of you."

"Pontifax and Junior were seen in consultation yesterday just before Junior went to the hospital for the wedding that didn't take place," the Giant went on. "They had the gray velvet case of diamonds open and Pontifax may have switched cases."

But Thompson shook his head. "Either those are good diamonds or they are such a close imitation of the other necklace that Junior himself would make a mistake. That isn't a casual imitation. It takes real work and time for a jeweler to imitate jewels. We haven't found a jeweler who has made an imitation."

"No. But Uncle Tim saw Junior and Pontifax together at least twice. And Uncle Tim gave me the lead that led me to discover that Pontifax had no connection with Magna Foods."

"Then what does he want with Uncle Tim? And the tomatoes?"

The Giant said slowly: "That I must see. Ask me in ten days."

The doorbell rang at that minute and I went to the front hall. The woman standing on the porch asked anxiously: "Is he here? Is Thompson Fenton here?"

"Yes. I'll call him." The woman looked like a beautiful but faded portrait. She looked a little like an older feminine version of Junior, I thought, with something of the strength of Junior's mother, the Duchess.

Behind me I heard Thompson. He said: "Maria," and in that moment I knew. This was the woman whose letter had been stained with Hugo's blood. This was the woman who was Hugo's real wife. Somehow she had managed to make it seem that I had murdered the man who was not really my husband.

I looked at her, standing slim and beautiful and tall on my front porch. Her eyes were narrow and green and her dressmaker suit matched them exactly. So did the scrap of furred hat above the smooth red hair.

This was Maria Thomassen.

"Will you come in?" I said, and took a step back, away from her.

"No. No, Maria. You must not come into this house. You have done enough." Thompson seized her arm. She laughed a little, and I think I have never heard a woman's laugh so enchanting. She was not young, but I could understand how a man could love her, even my Hugo.

And then I looked at Thompson's hand on her arm, and I thought: "Not—not Thompson, too."

I couldn't stand any more. I grabbed a coat from the hall stand and rushed out of the, house, leaving the door open behind me.

I heard Thompson calling me, but I couldn't stop. When I stopped running I was halfway down Main Street and people were beginning to stare at me more curiously than ever. I had on a fresh house dress, but my hair was just tossed up on the top of my head the way I usually wore it in the mornings. I had no hat or gloves or bag. My stockings were the cotton things I wore with house dresses and there was no glamor for my sensible shoes. I caught sight of myself in a drugstore mirrored window, and slowed down to a trot.

The neighbors probably thought I was insane. Maybe I was, a little. I stopped at the drugstore and ordered coffee. I gulped it down and bought a package of cigarettes and smoked one. Then I realized I didn't have my purse. I poked my hand into my coat pocket to see if I had any change to pay for the coffee and cigarettes.

In the pocket were crumbs of tobacco, a key ring and some papers. There was some change, too, and a couple of crumpled bills.

Then, and only then, I realized what I had done. I had taken the wrong coat. I had noticed before that Thompson had a coat of almost the same color as my old market coat. I had Thompson's coat instead of mine. I remembered now how shapeless and big the thing had looked when I'd seen it reflected in the mirror. I had been too bewildered when I dashed out of the house to have that uneasy unfamiliar feeling a woman usually has when she's wearing somebody else's clothes. I paid for the coffee and the cigarettes out of Thompson s money and then sat there, looking at the keys and the papers that I had pulled from the pocket.

Those keys looked very familiar, somehow. They weren't Thompson's. They were Uncle Tim's. Uncle Tim always carried twice as many keys as anybody else. He always had so many secrets to lock up.

That small key opened the door to Uncle Tim's print shop. It sounded like a refuge to me. Since I couldn't find Uncle Tim, I could at least stay in his shop, trying to conquer my own fears.

The key opened the door easily. The shop had the close pungent smell of ink and papers and dust, and I opened a window before I settled myself in Uncle Tim's big chair. The desk was so cluttered that I couldn't possibly have found room on it for another sheet of paper or can of ink.

There was even a row of tomatoes, neatly ripened, on a corner of the desk, and the batch of tomatoes that I had canned was standing among the papers. I hadn't even known that Uncle Tim had brought them down to the shop.

I tried to understand things one at a time so I wouldn't be too bewildered. You can stand almost anything if you don't try to believe too many impossible things at once.

Thompson had keys that belonged to Uncle Tim. That might mean that Uncle Tim had dropped them and Thompson had picked them up by accident. Or it might mean that Uncle Tim had given them to him for some reason. Or he might have stolen them in order to get into the print shop.

Marie knew Thompson. She might have known him earlier, when Hugo was killed, or she might have met him later, in Alaska or right in town. After all, she might have been there before. The Duchess was her sister and Junior her nephew.

Maria might have been the one who killed Hugo. She might have killed the Duchess. She might have killed Yates. But she couldn't possibly have poisoned Uncle Tim or Rosie because she wasn't anywhere around at the time. And if all of the trouble was connected, she couldn't possibly have pushed Natalie, because she hadn't been at the Zoo. But if Thompson and Maria had been working together—

then everything could be explained. Together they might have done everything.

Suddenly the telephone rang. I hesitated for a minute before I picked up the phone from its cradle. Junior's voice said: "I found the other necklace, Mr. Fenton. And we're going on with the wedding tomorrow,"

Mr. Fenton. The necklace. The wedding. I said nothing. I couldn't. I just felt stupid. Then Junior apparently became alarmed and I heard his phone shut down. The connection was broken.

TWENTY-THREE

The house was dark when I went into it, except for the light on the front porch and a little light burning in the hall. It might have been ten o'clock or eleven or midnight.

I turned out the lights and locked the door and went upstairs. I stopped outside of the boys' rooms and looked in long enough to make certain that both of them were asleep. Thompson's door was closed. Beyond it I could hear snores in two different keys, so I took it for granted that both Thompson and the Giant were there.

In my own room, I found myself locking the door against terror beyond my control. But in spite of all the panic I did feel better than before I had gone to the print shop.

I was in bed before I saw the note on the table beside me.

Dear Flo—
Don't believe everything you hear and only half you see. The lady is still beautiful but so are you. Take a look at yourself in a mirror some day when you get tired of cooking, canning, keeping house and advising relatives, ex-relatives, acquaintances and strangers.
Thompson

What did that mean? So he thought I could be blar-
neyed into believing him again! I had the impulse to get
up out of' bed and look in the mirror, but that was silly,
so I turned out the light and went tight to sleep in fewer
than five minutes.

I was awakened in the morning by Tommy and Donny
at the door. "Open up, Mom," Tommy ordered. "It's us
and we've got breakfast for you on a tray."

The breakfast was big and bountiful and I saw it with
delight at their thoughtfulness and a nagging worry that
I had neglected them. But they didn't seem any the worse
for what Tommy called "the gruesomeness of it all."

It seems that Junior and the beautiful lady had wept in
each other's arms, that the beautiful lady had visited Natalie in the hospital, that Natalie had changed her mind
again about marrying Junior and that Pop and the Giant
had gone off to the police station together, laughing. "And
Uncle Tim called up and said he'd have good news for us
today or tomorrow."

"And the Giant says he isn't any too sure that Pontifax
is European after all. It seems that some of the F.B.I. people have connections with him and he's working on our
side," Tommy finished, taking a piece of the toast and
strawberry honey he had so carefully spread for me.

Donny was drinking the orange juice. The children
know that I don't care for any breakfast except a cup of
coffee, but there's nothing they like more than an excuse
to bring it to me on a tray and then eat if themselves to
keep from wasting good food.

"The Giant says," mumbled Tommy through a mouth-
ful of toast, "that I'd make a good detective because I see
things clearly."

"I wish," I told him gloomily, "that you could see things
more clearly for me."

"Jeepers," said Tommy proudly, "all you gotta do now is to decide what you want to do first and do it. The Giant says that most people try to discover who murderers are, but it's the policemen who find most of 'em."

"In other words, trust the Giant and stop worrying."

Tommy nodded and Donny reached out for some more strawberry honey.

After the boys had gone off with the tray and I was getting ready to face the world, I kept thinking of what Tommy said. The kid had more sense than I did. Surely Thompson and Maria and Junior couldn't get away with anything much, even if one or more of them had committed a murder.

The house was a mess and it took me a couple of hours to give it a lick and a promise. Surely other women's children didn't drape trousers over chandeliers and themselves over newly laundered bedspreads. Surely other mothers didn't let their children keep puppies in the house and turtles on the mantlepiece in the living room. I was the wrong kind of mother. I didn't know enough about discipline, I thought, gathering up the debris from Donny's home work.

The telephone bell rang when I was on my way downstairs. It was Junior. He asked for Uncle Tim. I told him that Uncle Tim might be away or might be at the office, I didn't know. "I see," he said. "Well, Natalie and I have stopped squabbling. We're going to be married today."

I didn't remind him that he had said about the same thing the day before. I just said: "Are you sure she's strong enough to stand the excitement of having a lot of people there, Junior? Don't you think it would be better just to have the doctor and the minister and you?"

Junior said coldly, "If you don't care to be friendly, there is no need for you to come. But Natalie would like you to be there. She thinks a lot of you, Mrs. Fenton. And the rest of them, of course."

I'm not a woman for beauty shops, but this time I did go in to see what could be done for my face and hair. They tortured me with waving lotion and hair dryers and I didn't like what I saw when I came out. If you aren't the neatly waved type, then you aren't the neatly waved type. I washed out all the gooey stiffness and dried my hair in the back yard sunshine. It was really a little chilly to be drying hair outside, but I needed fresh air and sunshine after the beauty shop. I was outside when Uncle Tim went into the little greenhouse that he had put up around the tomato tank to protect it from the chilly winds that were beginning to blow at night.

He looked excited but old and very frail. He kissed me soundly, approved the waviness that the window was blowing into my hair and added, "Flo, we're going to be rich. We'll go to Mexico or South America and live like lords."

"But I don't want to live in Mexico or South America."

"Tut-tut—you can't stay here in this place all your life. Thompson's right. If we'd make you get up and go, you'd like it as soon as you'd given up rebelling."

I thought of something. "Uncle Tim, do you trust Thompson? You want him to stay with us?"

"Of course. You'll get along better now that you're both grown up. You wanted your way and he wanted his and so you couldn't help quarreling."

"But we didn't quarrel, Uncle Tim. We didn't quarrel at all. Thompson just up and left, and it was as much my fault as his."

Uncle Tim's perky head turned sharply. "What's that you say? Don't tell me that you're falling in love after all these years?"

"Of course not," I denied sharply. "Uncle Tim, where have you been, and are you staying home now?"

"I can't tell you anything until tomorrow—maybe not then. It took me less time than I figured, so I came back sooner. Are those kids married yet?"

"Junior and Natalie? Not yet. But the business about the necklace is all fixed up and they're going to be married today. How about going to the wedding? About three, and it's almost two-thirty now. My hair is dry and I'm going to make myself beautiful."

"You are already beautiful," my uncle said benignly, but he didn't look at me and I knew that he probably hadn't seen me clearly any time in the last twenty years. I belonged to him and therefore I was beautiful in his eyes.

TWENTY-FOUR

This time the wedding flowers were a little faded and Natalie looked not quite so lovely. She had been crying and there were pink spots high on her cheeks that didn't look like rouge. She seemed feverish, and I wondered why the doctor was permitting the wedding if she was so ill.

The doctor took me aside. "It's all a big mistake, Mrs. Fenton," he said. "I was telling your husband and his friend this morning that this girl should stay in the hospital for several months. She shouldn't have this wedding and she shouldn't leave the hospital, and if she persists in going ahead with it, it must be on her own responsibility. I can't approve of it."

"There is nothing that I can do. I'll try, if you want me to." I didn't succeed.

"Hi ya, Mrs. Fenton. Excuse me for being a little crazy yesterday. I do want to marry Junior. I guess I was delirious or something. I'm ready now."

This time the wedding went forward without a hitch. The bride sat up in bed against her pillows, with the filmy negligee draped around her shoulders and the bandages not showing at all.

When Natalie was Mrs. Stratton, we left her and Junior and the doctor in the hospital room and started down the street to our house. Uncle Tim was walking with me and

Thompson with the boys. Just ahead of us the Giant was strolling with Maria Thomassen. I realized then, that she must have been standing behind me in the hospital room. After all, she was Junior's aunt and wouldn't be likely to miss his wedding if she were in town.

Thompson joined us as we turned the corner into our own street and the boys ran ahead to join some of their gang waiting on the porch with the pups.

"Well, Unk," Thompson said, "get going all right? When do we leave for Mexico? Or did you decide on Brazil?"

"Before I forget it, Thompson," Uncle Tim said, "give me back my keys. And why did you open the box in the corner next to the Kelly press? That was private."

The keys. They were in my handbag at that minute! But I hadn't opened any box. I hadn't disturbed anything.

I'd meant to tell Uncle Tim about my period of rest in the shop but I didn't want to until we were alone.

Thompson put his hand in his coat pocket. I knew exactly what he'd find. Some loose change, some crumpled bills, crumbs of tobacco, and that was all. Those papers and keys were in the big envelope handbag so neatly tucked under my own arm at the moment.

Thompson turned pale and Uncle Tim turned red. "Give me those keys!"

Patiently Thompson explained: "I can't. I simply don't have them. They have disappeared from my pocket."

"When did you see them last?"

"Yesterday. I changed my coat when I came in. Remember I wore that checked coat with these pants. I got a splotch of wallpaper paste on the coat at Junior's house yesterday and put it down in the hall."

"Who was in the hall?"

"Well, while I was there—everybody. Even Maria, Junior's aunt." Thompson looked almost as bothered as I felt.

There was no real reason why I should have tried to put the papers and keys back into Thompson's pocket instead of just giving them to him or Uncle Tim with a word or two of explanation. It was simply a case of "being elaborate the way women are," as Tommy says.

But there was a reason for a sudden fear of Junior. He came and stood on the porch waiting. He said: "No. I won't come in. I've got to see Mr. Tim Fenton." His voice was menacing, the way it had been that night he threatened to strangle me. Uncle Tim took him out to the greenhouse and they sat there, on two old stools, talking vehemently. Junior got up from his stool and stood over Uncle Tim, who cowered before him. I started to go down to them, but Donny called me to say that the dinner was starting to burn, and I dashed into the kitchen to see whether the roast was scorching or whether I'd sifted a little flour into the oven instead of the roasting pan. By the time I got out, Uncle Tim and Junior weren't alone any more.

The beautiful Maria was with them, standing beside the tomato tank, looking up at the peach-colored tomatoes. While I watched, knowing that she was talking but not able to understand her words from a distance, Uncle Tim smiled and motioned toward the new stepladder behind the summerhouse. Junior got the stepladder and the beautiful Maria gracefully began to climb toward the top of the most beautiful tomato plant in the tank. It was as tall as a small tree, but then so were the rest of the plants in that tank. They were supported by big branches cut from forest trees and the fruits hung from the gnarled branches like some strange new exotic fruit.

I knew what Uncle Tim was saying, even if I couldn't hear his words. He would be telling how he had used potassium nitrate, calcium nitrate, magnesium sulphate, potassium phosphate, ammonium sulphate, ferrous sulphate and boric acid until, almost entirely by chance, he had experimented with the new nutrient that had made his tomatoes better than anything else in the field.

He was probably telling how some big corporation such as Magna Foods was going to pay him so much that we'd be going to Mexico or South America and live like kings.

But I couldn't hear what he was saying. And pretty soon he stopped talking and just looked up at Maria on the stepladder. She looked like something out of *Esquire* and I don't mean the cartoons.

Then I saw Maria lean forward on her step of the ladder and look intently at something attached to one of the branches that supported the tomatoes. After that Junior attracted Uncle Tim's attention by holding out a tomato and asking a question. I still couldn't hear the words but I saw Maria take something from the branch, tuck it quickly into her pocket, and then come down from the ladder. I saw that Uncle Tim was smiling at her and that when Junior looked at her she patted her pocket, with her hand, as if to reassure him. And in that moment I felt certain that the beautiful Maria now had in her possession something for which the Duchess had been killed.

They all came up to the house together. Maria and I looked at each other like strange dogs circling around each other before going in for the kill. But Uncle Tim and the boys were as obviously admiring as Junior. Thompson was noncommittal. He had a paintbrush and paint and was dabbing at a porch chair that had been needing paint for some three years.

"How about a little red enamel trim?" asked Donny. "I know where some is. I used it for my bookshelf last week."

He came down with the open can balanced on one hand. He was juggling it, in joyful imitation of one of his favorites on the screen.

I opened my mouth to say, "Be careful, Donny," as he passed Maria, and then I closed my mouth again, praying that he'd stub his toe as he passed her chair, the way I'd seen him stub it on the edge of the rug right there some dozen times.

Just as if he had been coached for the job, Donny tripped on the rug.

What that paint did to Maria's beautiful dressmaker suit is something that shouldn't happen to one of my dogs. I was an apologetic mother, obsequious about her child's tripping. I was an eager hostess grabbing the paint-stained coat from Maria's handsome shoulders in spite of her protests. And even the best pickpocket couldn't have done a better job of abstracting the flat gray velvet case from the big pocket than I did as I wiped as much paint as possible from the beautiful green fabric.

I was not, as the serials say, unobserved. Thompson saw me and held out his hand for the case. Meekly as a more carefully trained wife I handed it over. He tucked it behind the cookie jar on the top of the icebox and helped me with the paint.

"You must not—it is nothing." Maria grabbed the coat from me. Holding it gingerly, she gave us all some dazzling but absent-minded smiles and sped down the path toward the street. She was striding at least a foot ahead of Junior, talking excitedly all the way. When last I saw her, turning into Main Street, she was obviously very much excited and very angry.

Thompson and Donny were busy with the turpentine, and I got rags to wipe off the red paint from places where it should not have been.

Thompson had a splash of the paint on his sox and Donny had some on his pants, but I'd gladly have sacrificed more than that for the pleasure of seeing Maria's face when the paint splashed down on her.

"You are a cat, my dear wife," Thompson said. "You have sharpened your claws with red paint. If you had warned Donny in time the accident would not have happened."

"Accidents happen in the best of families," I said airily, with my eyes on the edge of the gray velvet case that peeped out from behind the cookie jar.

"The woman is not virtuous," said Uncle Tim with a sigh. "She is not the kind of person I approve of, but she is very beautiful."

"They probably said that about Cleopatra and Helen of Troy," suggested Thompson, wiping the last of the red paint from the table with the turpentined rag.

He gave careful directions to Donny and Tommy about what to do with both turpentine and rag, and Uncle Tim went along to make sure that they followed orders.

Thompson washed his hands that had already been cleaned of the paint with the turpentine, and went for the velvet case. "Two cents that it's the real necklace," he said. "Natalie got cheated on the deal."

But they all look alike to me. This might have been real and it might have been artificial. The important thing was, a little slip of paper from Uncle Tim's old notebook. I'd have known that notebook paper if I'd seen it in Timbuctoo. It had narrow blue and red lines, alternating. In Uncle Tim's neat printer's printing was a chemical formula and the words: "Peach—Tomato Tank."

Thoughtfully Thompson closed the velvet case. But the formula he put into his billfold which he then put in the pocket of his shirt.

TWENTY-FIVE

Before I could say anything, the telephone rang. Junior's voice asked: "Did my aunt drop anything out of her pocket while she was there?"

Thompson pointed to the case and shook his head. "You didn't see it," he whispered, knowing from my greeting to whom I was talking.

I obeyed, not knowing why, and put down the telephone receiver.

"Now we're in for more trouble. Why didn't you give it to him? It belongs to him."

"It belongs to Natalie, not Junior. The heir is supposed to give the jewels to his wife. The old lady's will said so."

"The Duchess?"

"No. Junior's grandmother. She left the jewels, not to Junior, but to Junior's wife. I think she knew that Junior would sell them as soon as they got into his hands and she wanted to keep them in the family."

"Then Junior may have gotten married just to have somebody to give the diamonds to." I couldn't make it add up to sense, but Thompson said:

"How about this: Junior has a duplicate of paste—a lot of people have them made so the real jewels can be kept in storage and just pulled out for big occasions. So he gives the imitation to his wife as per the grandmother's will and

145

then, with the real necklace in his hands, is ready to sell and get the cash."

"It's too mixed up for me. I don't understand all this messing around with jewels anyhow."

"Where are the jewels I gave you, Flo?" he asked then.

"They are upstairs, locked in my top dresser drawer."

"How long since you have looked at them?"

"Well, I wore the diamond wedding ring at a P.T.A. party five months ago because Tommy asked me to. And I saw the engagement ring then. The pin you gave me when Tommy was born is there, too, and that pearl necklace you brought home on our second anniversary." I was a little ashamed. He had always wanted to please me and I had accepted to much without even giving him the pleasure of letting him see me wear the things.

"Will you wear all the things this evening and dress up in your best bib and tucker? You and I are going out on the town tonight."

I agreed, thinking that it would probably be in very bad taste. But my neighbors couldn't disapprove of me any more heartily than they did already.

Thompson looked at the gray velvet box. "I'm going to make some calls. If you're going upstairs would you mind taking that velvet case up with you, please, and put it in my room? And while you're at it, you might drop the keys and my papers on my desk. See you later." He closed the door behind him and left me standing there with the case in my hand and with my mouth open.

I followed directions. I put the keys and the papers in the pocket without even looking at the papers. And I tucked the gray velvet case under Thompson's pillow where he'd be sure to feel it when he went to bed that night.

It had been so long since I had worn an evening dress that I hardly knew how to put one on. But my black velvet was classic, and so was the coat that went with it and the jewelry that Thompson had asked to wear.

"Matron in black velvet and pearls," I said, turning so he could see the way the skirt swished, when I met him in the hall after dinner.

"Lovely woman in black velvet and pearls," he corrected me. "And in engagement ring and wedding ring. And you've even worn the Tommy pin." He touched it gently, perhaps remembering as I did the day that he had brought it to me. He took a florist's box from the corner table. "The pin will fasten on your orchid," he said, and I busied myself with the flower.

I felt oddly excited, like a girl on her first date.

Thompson looked very handsome. He had a taxi ordered. "Funny," I said as we rolled down the street. "They don't like me to ride home from market in a taxi, but they haven't any objection to taking us out to dance. We are dancing?"

"If you'll put up with the vintage of my dancing—"

"My own is about the same."

I went into the hotel ballroom as frightened as if I were walking into danger deliberately.

And the first persons I saw were Junior and Maria. Maria was wearing a diamond necklace that, to my untutored eyes, looked like the one I had left under Thompson's pillow. But then I remembered the other one—probably Natalie had lent it to Maria.

Maria took immediate possession of both of us. "My friend Thompson and his charming wife. Welcome," she greeted us. "You will join us—yes? We have a table near the dancing floor. And there is what you call a floor show. They dance. They throw things. They fling themselves around. We see them closely, here at our table."

Maria was all in frosted silver with touches of jade. And the diamonds at her throat were made for her. The woman must have been only a few years younger than her sister, certainly older than I, but she was as beautiful as if she were just budding into womanhood, as the ads say. There was nothing of the faded portrait about her now. Some women are born to wear dazzling evening dresses. Maria was one of them.

I no longer wondered that Hugo had loved her. I only wondered how he had ever satisfied himself, even for a little while, with me as I had been twenty years before.

Maria kept looking at me even while she was talking to Junior and to Thompson. "I have not seen you before, Mrs. Fenton," she said. "I have heard of you many times. And you have heard of me or at least of my name. I have been told that you have even used my name as your own."

I nodded. "Yes. It was a stage name for me. I had no idea that there was really a woman by that name."

"Hugo did not tell you?"

"No. Hugo did not tell me."

"Good. He knew that you would have been jealous of me. You would have been right to be jealous of me, Mrs. Fenton. I," she added complacently, "was very beautiful twenty years ago."

I looked at the face and the hair, at the lovely lines of throat and arms and shoulders that showed no trace of age. "You are still very beautiful."

But Maria shook her head. "I have my moments," she said. "Some days I look all my years. This is one of my good nights. I am as old as your Uncle Tim, child. Would you know that? Tim and I went to school together, right here in this town. Tim and my sister and I."

"But you are so young—and your foreign accent . . ."

"My youth and my accent are alike artificial," she said. "Your uncle Tim and I are both nearly seventy. Look at me, child. Would you say that I am sixty-six years old?"

"Incredible," said Thompson. "I know it's true and I still don't believe it. You don't look forty. Tonight you look no more than thirty-five."

"There were belles in old France who had the secret of youth," she said with a sigh. "I tell myself I am like them. But I have no secret—except the tomatoes. I eat them always. All tomatoes. And now your uncle's tomatoes are wonderful. Tomatoes I need to make my health strong." She was drifting back into her oddly accented speech that had probably grown to be routine with her. "But the doctor told me I was allergic to them. I had to stop eating them until your uncle found a way to make these new tomatoes."

"And now the tomatoes are your beauty secret," Thompson finished for her.

Thompson had something up his sleeve. I knew that. He kept Maria talking for a while and then asked me to dance. Our dance was somewhat pedestrian, but that was my fault as well as his.

He danced with Maria after that, and they danced together not much better than Thompson and I had. But they talked and talked all the time they were dancing. Very earnestly. Junior kept turning to look at them.

"She's my mother's older sister," he said. "Would you believe it?"

"How is Natalie?" I asked. "And is your house ready for her?"

"The doctor says she can't be moved. He didn't want us to get married and now he doesn't want her to leave the hospital, although I'm fixing a whole suite for her and she can have a nurse with her every minute."

"She lent your aunt her wedding present, didn't she?" I asked, looking at the necklace around Maria's neck.

Junior shook his head. "That's just an imitation. My grandmother had two imitations that she gave to her younger daughters. And the oldest daughter got the necklace, the real one, when she had her first child."

"But you said that your aunt was the oldest—your mother was younger. There was a third daughter, too?"

"There was a third daughter. She has been dead for many years. Her necklace, an imitation, was lost. My aunt never had a child. She married twice, but had no child. So the second daughter, my mother, got the real necklace and my aunt got the imitation."

That accounted for three necklaces, not two. But which was the real one? And what did the necklace have to do with the murders?

I danced with Junior and then with Thompson again, and we were ready to sit down for the floor show when it was announced. "This is a magician," Maria announced, "and a very old friend of mine."

The spotlight sought out a man who stood up at a table beside the dancing space. He came forward casually, and bowed. Then he accepted a top hat from an attendant, clapped it on his head, lifted it, and tossed a white rabbit right on our table. I looked at the man's face. It was Pontifax.

TWENTY-SIX

I remembered the last time I had seen Junior and Pontifax in the wild Mack Sennett dash down the street. But now the two men were obviously good friends. The white rabbit was blinking up at me, frightened. It looked very young. I always like young things, puppies and even kittens, although I hate cats. The rabbit had a sprightly bow around its neck. Suddenly I saw that a note was tucked inside the ribbon. I took it out but I got no chance to read it.

Maria grabbed the paper from my hand. "It's mine!" she said, "You take my Hugo. You take my diamonds. But you shall not take my Pontifax."

"So it's out in the open," I said. Around us the audience was applauding Pontifax, who was doing something with bright chiffon handkerchiefs and a deck of cards.

Pontifax bowed, in his spotlight, and laughter and applause swept the room. The orchestra clashed into sound. People began to talk. Some dancers got up on the floor. But Maria and I sat there at, our table, glaring at each other while the men watched us.

"You killed my Hugo," Maria said. "I have hunted you for twenty years. The police shall know."

"You killed him," I countered. "I've told the police what I know. You tried to frame me but I got away. You killed him. Your letter—your knife—"

Maria darted her head forward in a motion like a snake. "I wrote no letter to him," she said. "When he told me that he loved you, I left. I told him that I had divorced him. He thought that he was free to marry you. I wrote no letter."

I looked at her green eyes and the firm hard line of her mouth, Either she was the best actress in the world or she was telling the truth.

"Then Hugo loved me. I—I couldn't understand that—not with you. You are so beautiful."

She looked at me intently. "But you were young," she said. "Young and very innocent. And this attracts a man like Hugo. He taught you to talk, to stand, to dress. You were his creation and he loved you."

"You say that you did not kill Hugo, Maria, and I know that I did not. Then who killed him?" We stared at each other, two women Hugo had loved.

"There was another woman. I knew that. A small young woman. Thin, eager, blonde. A grabbing woman. One who took everything she wanted. We used to call them 'Gimme girls' then. I never knew her name. Hugo called her Goldielocks. She hated me and she hated you."

I said: "You knew the woman? You saw her? It could not be—Natalie?"

Maria looked thoughtful and Junior looked shocked. "Natalie is young," he countered.

But Maria shook her head. "I talked to her doctor to-day," she said. "Natalie is older than you are, Junior. You are thirty. She is thirty-seven or eight. It is just barely possible that she could have been that other woman."

"But Natalie is not a blonde," I pointed out. "That other woman was a blonde. And she wasn't a woman—she was just a girl—seventeen or eighteen, at the time Hugo was killed."

"Have you looked at the roots of Natalie's hair?" asked Maria.

"Then she might have loved Hugo," Junior said softly, and I didn't like the look in his eyes. Menace again. Fury.

But Maria put her hand oh his arm. "I think," she said, "that Natalie now loves you very much. The doctor told me that when she was at her worst she called for you constantly." Junior's face cleared a little.

He said suddenly: "She couldn't have killed a man—not Natalie. Blood is abhorrent to her. In the ambulance, on the way to the hospital—" She shuddered at the memory.

Around us the music blared and the dancers talked and laughed. The lights were hot and bright.

Thompson hadn't said a word for a long time. Now he turned to Junior. "There may be some reason for her horror of blood. If when she was seventeen, she had killed a man, had seen him lying in his blood—" He stopped. I touched his arm and shook my head.

Maria straightened up and began to glow again, and I realized that another man was with us. It was the Giant, towering over us all.

"I have heard part of your conversation," he said. "We have established Mrs. Stratton's age, and we know that she was in New York twenty years ago. We know that she walked down Main Street just fifteen minutes after the murder of Mrs. Stratton Senior, so she may have been there, on the spot, when Mrs. Stratton died. She was also at your house when your Uncle Tim and Mrs. Yates were poisoned. But she was nowhere near when Mr. Yates was shot. And she certainly would not have pushed her own arm into the bear's cage at the Zoo."

"But," said Thompson thoughtfully, "the business about the bear may have been an accident. And Yates may have shot himself because of the discovery of the embezzlement and because Mrs. Yates was planning to divorce him."

The Giant sat up straight. "That would give us two coincidences," he said. "I don't believe in coincidences. Fate seldom arranges them. People do."

Junior stood up. "I can't stand this, any longer," he said. He planked a bill down on the table, anchored it with his glass and dashed out of the place. Maria watched him thoughtfully, but made effort to follow.

"I have another theory," the Giant said, waving away the waiter who offered him a card. "Junior himself may be guilty. He may easily have killed his mother. The motive is clear. He wanted to be rid of her domination. He wanted his money and his diamonds which he would never have if she lived."

"That is true," agreed Maria.

"He killed his mother. But the Yates' were looking out of the window and saw him so he had to kill them. And he was afraid that Uncle Tim might have seen him but was unsuccessful in poisoning him. Then later, Uncle Tim, proved by his actions that he knew nothing of the murders, so Junior felt safe."

"But Natalie? And Hugo? Junior loves Natalie. And he was only a child when Hugo died and would have no reason for wanting to kill him anyhow."

The Giant thought for a minute. "Natalie killed Hugo. And Junior found it out. The mangling of Natalie's arm might very well have been an accident. Junior and Natalie were teasing the bear. That has been established."

Just at that moment, the orchestra stopped and the spotlight focused again on Mr. Pontifax.

He went through a magic routine and then, in pantomime, suggested that he was hungry. One dancer came prancing in to offer a roast chicken—it looked like papier-mâché— Another offered a bouquet of vegetable, another an egg. Suddenly he produced an electric light bulb, lighted, and held it to his head, apparently to inspire an idea. Then he came over to our table, smiled wordlessly down at Maria, while the spotlight followed him, and took a bright peach-colored tomato from Maria's hair.

TWENTY-SEVEN

Pontifax bowed to Maria and handed the tomato to her. She looked at him, smiled, and then nonchalantly began to sprinkle salt upon the tomato and eat it from her hand, taking large greedy bites and looking very beautiful in the spotlight.

The crowd loved it. They began to call their waiters and demand that the magician create these new tomatoes for them, too. One drunk even came to our table and tried to snatch the tomato from Maria's hand, but she laughed at him and he went away. The waiters brought orders of tomatoes, and I heard people talking about their wonderful flavor, their magnificent unusual color.

Uncle Tim should have been there—the whole business would have been a delight to him. They must have been his tomatoes. Nobody else had tomatoes of that color and size and firmness. But why—

Maria answered me. "Next week," she said, "we go on the air in a new hour-long variety show for Magna Magnificent Tomatoes, the majesties of the crop. I am the star. Pontifax tries the first magic act on the air. We have found a way to carry some special illusions over the air. Your Uncle Tim has sold the formula and the seed to Magna Foods. We start building up consumer demand. In a very short time the product will be in the stores. Your Uncle Tim has made a fortune—thanks to me."

"To you? But he has been experimenting for years. He has been working with this formula for a long long time."

"Just the same," said Maria contentedly, "he owes the discovery to me."

The waiter had taken away the rabbit right after Pontifax had brought it, but now somehow I felt a sort of companionship with it. I felt that I had just about the mentality of a feeble-minded subnormal rabbit. That's how much I understood of all this nonsense.

We left not long after that and found Uncle Tim sleeping in his big chair on the porch. He awoke as we came up the walk.

"Local boy makes good, Uncle Tim. So that's why you gave us tickets to the dance." Thompson's grin was bright, even in the dim light of the porch.

Uncle Tim was proud. "Good show, huh? Pontifax working out all right? I still don't see how a magic act will go over the air, but they say they've got a new trick—some sort of audience participation thing. I'm printing the advertising. I wanted to do it all myself."

Thompson laughed. "You're the gardener, the creator, the printer, the artist and the chemist. 'Bride at the wedding, corpse at the funeral,' as somebody said about somebody else."

Uncle Tim said: "I'm going to be rich. I'll give Flo and the boys everything. You shall have the biggest car they make, Thompson. The boys will go to college. They'll be young princes."

"Hold on to your pipe dreams, Uncle Tim. We don't want all those things."

"I'll buy you jewels," Uncle Tim continued. "A diamond necklace like Natalie's. Pearls."

But Thompson shook his head. "Unk, have you lived with this woman of mine practically all her life and not discovered that she cares nothing for jewels? Tonight she is wearing jewelry for the first time in years. Isn't she wonderful?"

Just then I surprised myself by a large yawn. We all laughed and I went upstairs.

The next day I went to the hospital to see Natalie. She was sitting back against her pillows and a girl from a beauty shop was doing her nails.

"I ought to get a bargain rate, Mrs. Fenton, don't you think. Cleo is using only half as much polish."

Her smile trembled a little on her painted lips but she held her head high. As soon as the girl had gone we started talking, mostly about the way Junior was fixing over the house for her. "They're going to get me a new hand and arm in a little while," she said. "They do wonderful things nowadays. And if you have a diamond bracelet on a fake arm it may look prettier than a fake diamond on a real arm."

She laughed a little, sounding bitter and very very young. Yet she was thirty-seven or eight, almost as old as I. I'd been considering myself middle-aged for years, with my offspring growing up tall around me. And yet Natalie was a young girl in appearance and in manner.

"What do you think of Maria?" I asked. To my amazement, Natalie frowned and her lips curled into anger.

"I think she's done enough to me," she said. "She didn't have to come back to spoil our marriage."

"But she seems to approve of it. I know she does. She likes you."

Natalie laughed. "She hates me. She has broken up two romances of mine. But the third time is the charm. She can't take Junior away from me. Maybe that's why I picked her nephew this time, so she can't charm him away from me."

Then she changed back to some questions about the wallpaper in her new house and showed me some samples of house-gowns with draped sleeves that she was having made. "And I'm going to have a long fur cape this winter. Capes ought to be high style by next year. I can see it coming."

She was so matter of fact about the loss of her arm that I couldn't be otherwise. She seemed to take the position that it was a nuisance and an inconvenience, but she certainly wasn't going to let it ruin her life. She was the same person without the arm that she was with it and I admired both her spunk and her matter-of-factness. Both were important.

Maria came in as I was going out and we stood and chatted for a minute. Then Natalie looked from one to another of us and laughed. "I wish that Hugo could see us now," she said.

"Then you were the other girl?" Natalie shook her head.

"No. I was just a chorus girl on the outside looking in," she said. "But you've got the imitation diamonds and I've got the real ones now. Good-bye, both of you. Will you ask the nurse to come in, please, as you go out?"

Maria and I stopped for a coke. "Does that mean," she asked, "that Natalie is Goldielocks or that she just knew Hugo casually?"

"She likes Thompson," I said. "And she liked Hugo. So did you, Maria. And so did I."

"We're fated to like the same men," Maria said. "Even Tim. I almost married your Uncle Tim. Then your parents died and left you to him, and I wasn't taking on any ready-made family."

"Three men." I went on sipping my coke.

"And I," said Maria thoughtfully, "didn't really care enough about any of them to give up my freedom for them.

I'm sixty-six, child, and I still wouldn't let any man tell me when to go and come."

"You married Hugo," I reminded her.

"Yes. But it wouldn't have lasted, even if he hadn't met you. Hugo wanted to recreate his women on his own pattern and I liked my own personality better than the one he wanted to give me. That cooked my goose with Hugo."

We went on talking about the new radio hour and Pontifax and the tomatoes. I told Maria the tale about how Pontifax and Junior had run down the street, and she laughed until she cried but couldn't understand why Pontifax should have been chasing Junior.

The Giant found us there together, in the drugstore. "Good detective work," I told him.

"Well, I thought of where I'd go after leaving an hysterical female. A saloon didn't sound like you, so I though that you might substitute a coke for a Scotch and soda. This is the drugstore nearest the hospital."

"Simple, Watson. We've just about decided that there weren't any murders."

"You are one third right." The Giant deliberately reached into the holder for a straw and took a sip of my coke. "Yates was not murdered. We found fingerprints on that gun that was in your yard. Mrs. Yates' fingerprints."

"But she didn't murder him?"

"No. The position of the fingerprints indicates that she picked up the weapon and threw it out into your yard. The divorce and the embezzlement were enough to make any man commit suicide. But the suicide clause in the insurance policy made his wife try to make the suicide look like murder."

"And now she is dead and nobody gets the insurance anyhow." Poor Rosie.

The Giant shook his head. "She left a will and some insurance of her own, too. She left everything to your husband, Thompson Fenton."

TWENTY-EIGHT

As each little thread of the plot was straightened out, more snarls came to take its place. Thompson. It was natural, of course. She had loved him, had planned to go back to him. She had no family, no children.

"What does my husband say?"

"That he doesn't want the money. What could he say? He knows that this gives him an excellent motive for the murder of Mrs. Yates. We have evidence now that he quarreled with Mr. Yates some hours before Mr. Yates killed himself. We have evidence that he was hidden by Mrs. Yates before the murder of Mrs. Stratton. We have evidence that he was in the attic just before we went there looking for him, after the death of Mrs. Yates. It is entirely possible that he was there, too, the night the shot came through your attic window, Mrs. Fenton."

I felt myself shivering. The coke was distasteful to me. I pushed it away. The room seemed suddenly very close. "Natalie—" I asked.

The Giant said: "We don't know about that. He may have bumped her. He may not. Anybody might have bumped her, even your Uncle Tim or Junior or you, Mrs. Fenton. And there is still the possibility that I mentioned once before. Mr. Fenton may have killed Hugo Kiphart."

"I don't believe a word of it," said Maria. "Thompson laughs at things and runs away. He wouldn't kill anybody. He can't even set a rat trap or kill a rabbit. I know. I've heard him kidded by some trappers we knew years ago, when I was singing in Alaska. Thompson is no killer. Flo Fenton, don't you have any faith in your own husband? If you don't, you may as well hand him over to some other woman who has. I'd take him myself if I were fifteen or twenty years younger."

"No woman would have a chance," I told her, grateful but shaky, "if you really wanted her man."

"That would explain everything," the Giant said.

"But why would he kill the Duchess?"

"Because she learned of the early murder of Hugo and felt that the murderer was Thompson. I've already told you. Look, Mrs. Fenton, I've had evidence built up against every one of these people and you spoil one case for me after another."

"You'll be thinking next," said Maria thoughtfully, "that Flo Fenton herself is the real murderer. I can still remember that satin nightgown spotted with blood and the slipper prints in blood that you left on the floor of the lobby."

Some warning flash in my mind told me: "Something's wrong here." I thought back. She couldn't have seen the gown spotted with blood. I had taken it with me. I had hidden it in the suitcase in our attic. Except for the moment after Donny was born when Thompson had seen it, the gown had not been seen by anybody.

Unless—unless Maria had seen it before I'd come back to the hotel. Unless Maria herself was the murderer.

Maria lit a cigarette. "If you murdered Hugo," she said, "surely you have no reason to fear the law now. Don't they outlaw murders after ten years, or is that debts?"

I had to get the Giant alone to tell him about the night-gown. I said: "I'm going to my husband. Will you please come with me, Giant? Good-bye, Maria."

I waved casually and handed the girl some change for our cokes and was out of the place in a minute. The Giant loped after me. I sped down the street but waited at the corner. "I've got something important to tell you," I said.

With satisfaction, he told me, "I thought you might have. As soon as your husband was arrested."

"Is he arrested?"

"Well, maybe not quite. But he's sort of in protective custody. I left him on your front porch playing gin rummy with your Uncle Tim. What do you have to tell me, Mrs. Fenton?"

"Maria is the murderer." I told him about the night-gown. About the footprint in blood that the old hotel clerk had mentioned such a short time before, about the diamond necklace and the way that Maria had had to hand it over when Junior was born, how she had taken it from the tomato tank stakes and how I had taken it from her when Donny spilled the paint.

It was a long story but he didn't interrupt. We were at Uncle Tim's house by the time it was told.

Uncle Tim and Thompson had stopped playing and were beginning to get restless. "I know. You're hungry," I said. "All of you stay here and I'll see what I can dig up in the kitchen."

I fixed up a big plate of things I had in the icebox and the relishes and fruits I'd canned that summer. I kept thinking, when I added my chili sauce, how much prettier the catsup was that I'd made from Uncle Tim's tomatoes.

I had a bowl of salad stuff from the garden and some of my Roquefort dressing was ready in the box. I put the cof-fee on and called Thompson to help me carry in the trays.

He came into the kitchen and closed the door. "Flo," he said, "I've got to make you understand that I didn't do these things. Even if everybody else thinks I did, you'll know, won't you, that I didn't?"

I went closer to him and looked into his eyes. And then suddenly I was in his arms. After all those years his arms were around me again. And this time I wasn't pretending that it was Hugo. This time it was Thompson himself who was holding me, Thompson who was kissing me, Thompson whose heart was pounding close to mine.

I was crying a little when he released me. I, Flo Fenton, who never cry. I was loving him more than I'd ever known that I could love a man.

My days of being an emotionless, serene, middle-aged housewife and mother and niece were over. I was a woman in love and I didn't care who knew it. Tommy and Donny came in and just stood there, looking at us. I was trembling, I know, and I think that Thompson was, too.

Tommy said: "It's all right, Pop?" and Thompson answered shakily:

"It's all right, kids. We're a family again."

The kids helped us carry in the food and set the table. Thompson kissed me again behind the dining room door and Tommy saw and obviously approved. We ate supper, and even the Giant managed to stow away plenty. My newfound love didn't seem to affect my appetite. But I did catch myself feeling a little sorry for every woman who wasn't married to Thompson, and they say that's a pretty good symptom of a happy marriage.

This time the kids helped carry out some of the supper stuff and then vamoosed to the yard when Thompson told them to. I could see right then that the house was going to get some much needed discipline.

The Giant said: "Your wife is worried that I'm arresting you for murder, Fenton."

"Are you?" Thompson smiled at me and I almost spilled my cup of coffee. "Well, I might be guilty. But anybody might be guilty."

The Giant took from his pocket a small knife wrapped in a piece of white paper and put it down on the table. Then he took another knife from my table and put it down on the paper too. They matched, exactly.

"The knife that murdered the Duchess, Mrs. Fenton," said the Giant, "seems to belong to you."

TWENTY-NINE

"The knife is mine," I admitted. "But my education in knife-throwing has been sadly neglected."

Everybody was looking at me. Thompson came a little closer and put his hand on my shoulder. "Nobody really thinks you're a murderess, Flo," he reassured me.

"Flo doesn't murder people. She feeds 'em," Uncle Tim said in his usual mild tone with his normal chuckle.

The Giant said: "It's good food, too. How do you explain the knife, Mrs. Fenton?"

"I don't. Anybody could have taken it. People run in and out of here all day long. It's like a railroad station with eating concessions. The boys could have taken it outside and left it there for the murderer to pick up and throw."

"I might have taken it out myself, or Thompson might have," Uncle Tim said. "And Junior and Natalie were eating tomatoes out in the yard one day. Junior came in and got a knife—maybe this one. That was before the Duchess was killed and before Natalie was hurt. That knife might be the one."

"Thanks, Uncle Tim. He doesn't really think I'm a murderer. He just accuses everybody in turn of being guilty. He'll accuse you next, or Maria, or Junior."

"Maria. She is a possibility," Uncle Tim said.

"She wasn't here when her sister died."

"But she was. She was here at three o'clock on the day that the Duchess was killed. I saw her, talking to Junior and Mr. Pontifax and Natalie right here in the summer-house. And about that time the Duchess came along."

I sat up straight and so did the Giant. "You told me that you didn't see the Duchess before three-fifteen. And you didn't tell me that you saw Maria at all on that day." The Giant was stern.

Uncle Tim shrugged his shoulders. "You didn't ask me. You didn't say a word about Maria."

The Giant held his head with both hands. Then he sighed and said: "Why did I ever want to be a policeman? Why didn't I take a nice easy job like ditch-digging or flying kites from skyscraper roofs? Look, Mr. Tim Fenton, are there any other questions I have failed to ask you? Have you any other answers hidden in your high and mighty brain?"

Uncle Tim chuckled. "Well, I don't know. I saw Maria and I saw Junior and Natalie. Any of them could have killed everybody, but I am not an expert on murder. I can tell you anything about hydroponics. I've tried all the methods, even that simplified formula with potassium nitrate, monocalcium phosphate, magnesium sulphate, iron sulphate and water." We were startled, and Uncle Tim continued: "I can tell you about printing. I'd advise you to use Caslon Oldstyle type on a rough finish antique paper. But I'm not an expert on murder, with knives, poison or stepladders."

"Very funny," said the Giant. "Now if you will excuse me, I have an appointment with Mr. Pontifax."

After he left and Uncle Tim went up to his room, Thompson and I sat on the porch holding hands. We didn't talk much. There was so much to say that we didn't say much of anything.

Thompson asked once: "You know why I had to go away? You know why I found somebody simple and stupid and bold and shrill and obvious, like Rosie?"

I did understand. Poor Rosie. "Even when I saw you again, I wanted her," Thompson confessed. "I was afraid of letting myself love you again and be hurt. I've always run away from things that hurt. I think I'm a coward, Flo. Except that I don't think I'd ever try to run away from you again. It's hell to love a woman and know that she's in love with a dead man."

I touched his cheek with my hand. "I'm in love with a live man now, Thompson. He's very much alive, darling, and so am I."

Thompson said: "I kissed Rosie, that night she came here, after her husband killed himself. She told me that he did. She told me that she had thrown the gun over here. But the police had it by that time. When I kissed her after seeing you, I knew that I'd have to run away again. I couldn't marry her again, loving you."

"You're a bigamist, Thompson."

"I guess I am, in a way. But we were very careless about previous marriages up there, and I think I've atoned for it. I can't ask you to forgive me. But I do love you—very much."

Uncle Tim came in while we were sitting there and looked at us sharply. "Is it Junior, do you think?" he asked. "Or Maria?" There was something a little sly about his mention of her, as if he knew just a little more than he had told us and the Giant.

I began to wonder then if Uncle Tim, for the sake of his old love, had hidden some facts that would prove Maria guilty of the murder. I hesitated about whether to tell him about her mention of the gown and then saw that he seemed very tired. He went to bed early and so did the kids, and we were sitting in the living room, Thompson on the couch and me on the footstool at his feet, when the telephone rang.

"I saw Junior," said the Giant's voice, "and Natalie is at home with him and with his Aunt Maria. I know that it's late. But they want to know if all of you could drop over here tonight for a little—well, a little gathering. Tell your uncle that Pontifax is going to be there, too."

I called upstairs to Uncle Tim and he reluctantly agreed to go with us. I heard him grumbling as he put on a clean shirt and brushed his hair. Uncle Tim did hate to go out in the evening.

The boys were still awake. I suggested that they go to bed but take a couple of the puppies upstairs with them. "You're big enough to be alone in the house all night, if necessary," I told Tommy, "but your father and I will be home in an hour or two, I think."

"Is Uncle Tim going too?"

Uncle Tim's voice answered as he came out of his room and closed the door. "Uncle Tim is going under protest," he said. "I don't see any sense in going out at night just because a woman comes home from a hospital where she should be staying. That bear should have taught her more sense."

Thompson drew me out into the kitchen with him when he went to turn out the lights and lock the kitchen door. "Darling," he whispered, "promise me you'll love me, no matter what happens?"

I was a little more frightened than I had been. I kept thinking of Maria. I kept wondering about the bloodstain on the satin nightgown. I kept thinking about the small white vanity case with the bloody fingerprint on it. And then suddenly I remembered, from the emptiness of twenty years, pushing something out of the way so I could read that bloodstained letter without lifting it up in my hands.

That small square white thing might easily have been a vanity case of the kind that girls used then. Not mine. Maria's, possibly. Or one belonging to Goldielocks, who-ever she was.

"I've just remembered, Thompson," I whispered. "That vanity case may have been in the room, lying across the letter, weighting it down. I may have pushed it aside. I think that I did, so I could read the letter. My fingerprint may be on the case. Oh, Thompson, you'd better promise to love me, even if they arrest me for a murder I didn't do."

I had only the vaguest idea about the ways that evi-dence could pile up to prove a person guilty of murder, and this didn't help me. But Thompson's arms around me and Thompson's kiss did help.

Uncle Tim was waiting for us on the front porch. "A lot of nonsense," he said testily. "People ought to go to bed and sleep at night."

We walked. It was only a few blocks. None of use said much except once when Uncle Tim asked: "Ever find the keys, Thompson?" and Thompson answered by handing them to him.

When we got to Junior's house it was all lighted up. Paint and paper and bright lights helped make a gay place out of a gloomy one. Natalie looked very fragile and very lovely as she reclined on a blue velvet lounge with a shock-ing pink blanket tossed over her. Her empty sleeve was hidden, and the hand she offered us was neatly manicured.

Maria looked beautiful and rather tired and older. She kissed me and then went on to kiss Uncle Tim and Thomp-son too.

I heard her say to Uncle Tim: "It could be our silver anniversary. Or is it diamonds? Thirty-five years ago to-night we planned to be married. Remember Tim?"

He took both hands and looked into her eyes and I saw her blush a little. We all settled down, the lights bright and silence strong between us. The Giant began:

"I have some things to tell you, and other things to ask you. Bradfield is here and a few more of my colleagues. They are in the next room. I want to have a sort of consultation tonight, and by the time we are finished, I think that we shall know who the murderer is."

Thompson said uneasily: "Like the last act of a farce."

The Giant nodded. "The name of the farce is 'Twenty Years Later,'" he said. We all looked at him. He was standing straight and very tall beside the door. Uncle Tim, next to him, looked like an insect of a man, thin and brittle and tired. But Maria was glowing now, as if all her fatigue and age had passed in just a few minutes.

"I shall like this farce," said Maria. "Pontifax must remember it. We can perhaps use some of it in our radio hour."

But the Giant shook his head. "Pontifax already remembers," he said.

THIRTY

"The knives were very sharp," said Pontifax. "But they had learned their lessons well. I was not afraid that they would hurt each other."

The Giant seemed to know what he was talking about, even if I didn't. The Giant took a knife from his pocket. Then he reached into another pocket and took out a case. In this there were other knives, just like the first, and just like the ones I used for peeling potatoes.

"Will you give us a demonstration, Mr. Pontifax?" asked the Giant.

"Let me act as subject," offered Uncle Tim. He stood stiffly against a door and Mr. Pontifax chose a knife, aimed it directly at Uncle Tim and let the knife go. I expected to see my uncle drop dead at our feet, but Mr. Pontifax and Uncle Tim were both quite calm and scientific.

"We did it years ago," Maria said. "My sister, Mrs. Stratton, and Tim and Pontifax and Hugo. We all learned from an expert. It was a stage trick. We were all good at it."

With the knives around his body, Uncle Tim smiled. "It was fun, in the old days, when we were young."

"But some of you were younger than others," said the Giant. "Hugo was younger and handsomer. And he wanted Maria and he took her from you."

"That was many years ago," said Uncle Tim. The pattern began to form. The endless moments ticked on. I could hear a clock somewhere. I have never liked clocks.

"Then Flo went away, too. You lost Maria and you lost Flo. You went to New York to find Flo and you discovered that Hugo had taken her away, too, after he had already taken and discarded the beautiful Maria."

I felt that I had to hold back time, to make the Giant understand that things hadn't happened like that. "You can't accuse Uncle Tim." I was panicky.

The Giant looked at me with pity in his eyes and I began to realize that Uncle Tim might have lived in the little house for all those years with secrets in his heart, too. I had hidden tragedy. Maybe he had hidden his own tragedy.

I found myself moving a step toward him. But his expression wasn't even familiar any more. This wasn't Uncle Tim. The Giant spoke gently, to me, not to the rest.

"This time I am sure. It's been a long time, but we have been lucky. The pieces of evidence fit together neatly. We have a case." I didn't understand exactly, but Uncle Tim did, and I could see him wilt into a gray shadow of himself.

The Giant said something about warning him that anything he said could be used against him and then he began to talk directly to Uncle Tim. He referred now and then to a little paper in his hand, as if he had noted down the important details. Like a grocery list, I thought, and found my teeth chattering with cold as I listened.

"When you went into Hugo's room, he wasn't alone," the Giant said. "There was a girl with him, a girl who was trying to persuade him not to marry Flo. She didn't know that they were already married until you went in, without knocking, with your sharp little knife in your pocket." A sharp little knife. I felt that I could never peel a potato again.

Uncle Tim looked straight at the Giant, appearing even a little proud, like a triumphant insect. The Giant said: "You showed her the wedding dress and veil, so she knew that they were already married?" It seemed a question, and Uncle Tim nodded.

"You had sent Flo to the Waldorf so she'd be out of the way?" It was another question, and Uncle Tim nodded again. But he didn't look at me.

"With Flo out of the way, you thought you'd be alone with Hugo, to kill him as you had planned. But here was a girl, a silly little girl, so blind with love and anger that she hadn't even seen Flo's dress and veil on the bed until you pointed them out to her. The girl left, frightened, when you demanded to see Hugo alone. But she didn't go far. We know."

I was back suddenly in that hotel corridor, waiting for my Hugo who would never come, and it took Thompson's voice to return me to the present.

"Don't care so much, darling. I've known—I've tried to save him—and you."

Thompson seemed suddenly the only person in the room who was alive. The rest were shadows, talking or silent. Uncle Tim, standing against the wall, surrounded by the little sharp knives, was like a poster of a circus act.

"That girl. Who—" My words came out almost as a whisper. I looked at the women, but they were just shadows, too.

The Giant said to Uncle Tim: "You killed him with that little sharp knife, throwing it almost from the door, so you could get away in a hurry."

I remembered the note, and the room. "But—"

But the Giant knew, somehow, and Uncle Tim's set face confirmed it. "You threw the knife and you killed him, just as you killed the Duchess later, after you had carefully set the stage for murder with the stepladder and the poisoned tomato. You were suddenly afraid that the poison would take too long or the broken stepladder would just mean hurting and not killing the enemy who had discovered your murder of Hugo and was trying to take everything away from you—even the tomato discovery that might make millions."

"She had no right," Uncle Tim said matter-of-factly. "She was a malicious old woman and she had no right to blackmail me."

"Her life was her own and you took it from her," the Giant said. "You murdered her—three times you murdered her," he added. "When you saw her coming, you put the poisoned tomato where it would tempt her. You put the stepladder right where she'd stand on the broken step to get the tomato. She had done it before. She had stolen every other tomato on that branch before. And you stole them back again. We found her casserole with the spoiled tomatoes in your workshop, next to the saw that had probably been used on the stepladder. But we let ourselves be talked into the idea that this was a plant. It wasn't. We should have kept you in jail when we had you there."

Uncle Tim's voice was calm and reasonable, as if he were explaining to the children why they shouldn't go swimming right after dinner. "But I had to kill her, and I didn't dare wait to see if the ladder and the poison would work. She might have lived long enough to talk. She knew about Hugo."

"Two cases against you," the Giant said, "and either would do to put you where you should be. You left Hugo, knifed before he knew what hit him. Then you left the hotel but waited around outside until Flo should return. You wanted her to come back to you and ask for refuge. It must have been gratifying when she pretended to have forgotten all about her life away from you—her life with Hugo. You knew there was no real amnesia, of course.

Only a bewildered girl like Flo would ever have attempted to fake. And it was just luck that she got away with it for all this time."

"She came back," Uncle Tim said with satisfaction, looking at me for a second. Then he froze into indifference. Odd. How could he be indifferent?

"But two women visited the room after Hugo was dead and before Flo came back. Maria went to leave a note for him. She dropped the note when she saw the body. Then she saw the bloodstained nightgown. If she had not been there in that five minutes she could not have seen the nightgown, and we know she saw it. And she didn't leave the building until after Flo left or she could not have seen the bloody footprint Flo left on the paper in the lobby."

Maria moved restlessly. She looked old but very beautiful. "That room," she said, "and all that blood. And the gown. And the footprint. I thought that Flo killed him. I always thought so."

The Giant shook his head and looked reassuringly at me for a minute. "Not after you saw the knife," he told Maria. "Flo didn't know how to throw a knife. But you didn't tell the Duchess until a short time ago, after you saw the girl again—Hugo's other girl—Goldielocks."

I found myself looking at Natalie.

But the Giant shook his head. "Not Natalie," he said. "Rosie Yates. She wanted to make trouble for Maria and for Flo, too. She always hated Flo. That's why she tried to take Thompson away. She loved him later, I think, but not at first. There was no coincidence about the meeting of Rosie and Thompson. Rosie planned it all that way and deliberately bought that house next to Flo's so she could grab Thompson if he ever came back."

Thompson made some little sound but I couldn't look at him. Uncle Tim's face was politely curious as if he were listening to neighborhood gossip.

"Rosie put Maria's letter under the body and deliberately dipped the wedding veil in the blood. She had nothing of Hugo's to leave there except the little white vanity case he had given her as a farewell present when he married Flo. She dropped the case on the letter to hold it close to the body so nobody could miss it. By chance Flo, when she came, touched the vanity case and left a fingerprint."

"These things happened twenty years ago. How can you prove them?"

"I shall not need to prove them," the Giant said, "A man can die but once although his murders are many. You killed Rosie, too, when she became troublesome, and then took a little poison yourself, to fool me."

"I shall not die for these murders," Uncle Tim said clearly. "Why should I kill? I shall have money—lots of it. I shall have everything a man wants. I shall travel—in Mexico, in South America."

But the Giant shook his head. "You will stay here. We have enough evidence for a case. And your words would convict you, if there were no evidence."

It was all so artificial, so unreal. The circus poster effect was still there. Uncle Tim stood, immobilized by Mr. Pontifax's knives, as if he had been tied to the door.

At that minute, Uncle Tim moved swiftly.

He twisted one hand just trifle. He seized one sharp little knife that Mr. Pontifax had thrown and poised it in his hand.

"I throw very well," said Uncle Tim, somewhat smugly and without panic. "Perhaps you'll get me, but the Giant dies first. I'm a very small man to kill such a big one. Hugo was big, too, and the Duchess. But they died." He slipped out of the ring of knives on the door. He raised his hand.

The Giant merely nodded to Mr. Pontifax. And in that moment, another knife flew through the air and Uncle

Tim's hand dropped his knife as blood streamed from his fingers.

The rest was a hodge-podge of noise and terror.

And that was how everything happened. After twenty years. I couldn't believe it, even when I knew it was true. The Giant had been right in the first place and he should have kept Uncle Tim in jail. Then Rosie would still have been alive. But he let me talk him into a momentary belief in Uncle Tim's innocence and he brought Uncle Tim home.

Uncle Tim had sawed the stepladder step, had hung the poisoned tomato right where the Duchess would be sure to grab it when she climbed the stepladder he had left temptingly near. And then he had thrown the knife that killed her when he had been afraid the Duchess might survive the fall or the poison. He wanted to be triply sure. Uncle Tim had always been a thoroughly cautious man.

The Duchess had been told about the first murder by Maria, and had blackmailed Uncle Tim. She wanted those tomatoes and the cash and fame that would come with them. And she wasn't any too particular about the ways she took to get them.

It took me days to learn everything and even now I'm not too sure about what the diamonds had to do with the murders. I think that Uncle Tim had needed money to perfect some of his chemical experiments and had taken the set on the Duchess' body. Those were the real ones, I believe, and the rest were artificial. Junior hadn't shown them to the jeweler. He was afraid that he might be told that they were false and his ego was too warped to stand that. I didn't get the details about the rest of the diamonds, but the Giant did explain. Uncle Tim, for some reason, had tried to make it appear that Natalie had stolen the real ones. And Natalie hadn't confessed that hers were artificial because she thought she knew where the real ones were and might be able to get hold of them. If I sound a bit mixed up, it's because, as Thompson says, the diamonds weren't really important. They were just a sideline to murder. I don't think that Maria ever knew whether it was the real ones or an artificial necklace that she found and that I took away.

Rosie's murder wasn't so carefully planned. Uncle Tim seemed oddly resentful when he finally recognized Rosie after she had tried to get money from him to get away from her crook of a husband. It was easy, though, to poison her drink and then to put just a little poison in his own drink and pretend to be sicker than he really was.

And Natalie's accident was really an accident. Uncle Tim had tried to push Junior toward the cage after he had teased the bear. Junior knew more than he ever told. But Natalie got in the way. And instead of Junior's head, it was Natalie's arm that got too near the bear.

Thompson says that all my explanations don't really explain anything. He says that I haven't made it clear that Uncle Tim killed Hugo because he had taken the only two women Uncle Tim had ever loved—Maria and me. He says that I haven't even made it clear that he killed the Duchess because she threatened to tell about Hugo's murder unless he let her walk away with the formula for the hydroponic tomatoes.

Perhaps Rosie saw Uncle Tim murder the Duchess. We never knew. Maybe he just killed her because of the blackmail of the first murder.

I try not to think of that night when Thompson and I walked home together, slowly, to the house where the boys lay sleeping. Uncle Tim would never come back to the house. His old coat was hanging on the rack and I put it in the cupboard, wondering if I'd ever see it again on him.

Thompson made coffee and we sat down on the porch in the dark.

"He was so good to me, Thompson," I said. "I still can't believe it."

Thompson was gentle but very certain. "He was good to you because he felt that you belonged to him. It was right for him to treat you gently because you were, in a way, a part of him. Even then, he was willing to sacrifice you if he had to. He was willing to let everybody think that you were guilty. That box in his print shop held the blood-stained wedding dress, the one he said he had destroyed. And the other day he took down the bloodstained shoes that matched the footprint on that paper in the hotel lobby. The police still had that. And the night you went to the attic and left him sleeping on the porch—or pretending to sleep—he went up to the boys' tree-platform and tried to shoot you. He thought it would be a confession of guilt. He could say that you told him you had killed the Duchess because she knew you had killed Hugo." Thompson seemed very sure of his facts and I never asked him how he knew.

"I don't believe he would hurt me. Not me."

"But you must believe me," Thompson said. "I was in Rosie's attic, watching over you. I did go to New York, but I came back right away. I couldn't let anything happen to you, Flo. Not now. Not now that you're mine, instead of Hugo's."

And I knew, too, that he loved me in spite of everything, and I loved him.

He went away because he wouldn't share me with Hugo's memory. And he came back because he suddenly realized, after all those years, that he'd rather be unhappy with me than happy with any other woman.

I remembered then how he had left after the boy was born. I remembered his face that had told me nothing and his voice that had not told me much more.

And he has taught me to remember Uncle Tim only as he was during those years when he was so kind to a little orphan girl. That Uncle Tim will never die, although the strange murderer with the mask of Uncle Tim's face has long since paid the penalty for his crimes.

But I shall never peel a potato without a little shudder, and Thompson brings home all the little gadget peelers on the hardware store shelves so I won't have to use that sharp little knife in the kitchen cabinet drawer.

About the Author

Minna (Feibleman) Bardon (1900-1974), graduated from Hughes High School in Cincinnati, Ohio, and worked her way through college at the Jewish Settlement community center. She sold her first story when she was 12, and wrote a number of romance, detective, children's, and science fiction tales before writing ten books (at least four of which are mysteries). She married Emanuel Bardon in 1931 and had twin daughters and a son. She worked in advertising, then for *Writer's Digest*. She also wrote book reviews for the Cincinnati *Enquirer*. After her husband died in 1958 she became a social worker, helping women find jobs.

Also Available
Coachwhip Publications
CoachwhipBooks.com

THE BRIDE DINED ALONE

VERA KELSEY

Coachwhip Publications

WHISPER MURDER!

VERA KELSEY

CoachwhipBooks.com

SALLY WOOD

Coachwhip
Publications

MURDER
OF A
NOVELIST

DEATH
IN LORD
BYRON'S
ROOM

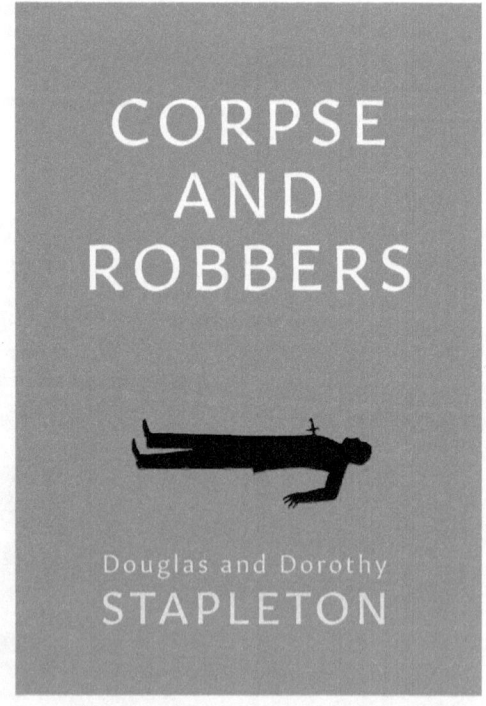

CORPSE
AND
ROBBERS

Douglas and Dorothy
STAPLETON

CoachwhipBooks.com

HELEN BURNHAM

THE MURDER OF
LALLA LEE

—

THE TELLTALE
TELEGRAM

Coachwhip
Publications

Scarecrow

EATON K. GOLDTHWAITE

CoachwhipBooks.com

Jack Dolph

MURDER MAKES THE MARE GO

Coachwhip
Publications

THE RUMBLE MURDERS

Henry Ware Eliot, Jr.

CoachwhipBooks.com

MURDER OF
THE HONEST BROKER

WILLOUGHBY SHARP

Coachwhip
Publications

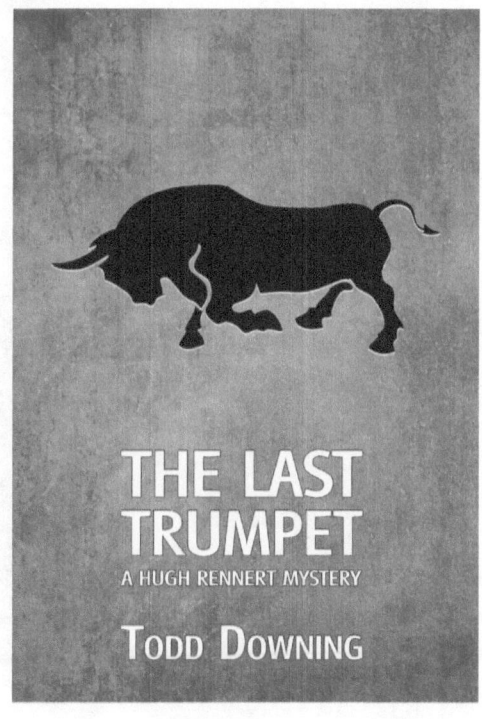

THE LAST
TRUMPET
A HUGH RENNERT MYSTERY

TODD DOWNING

CoachwhipBooks.com

A Matter of Iodine

David Keith

Coachwhip
Publications

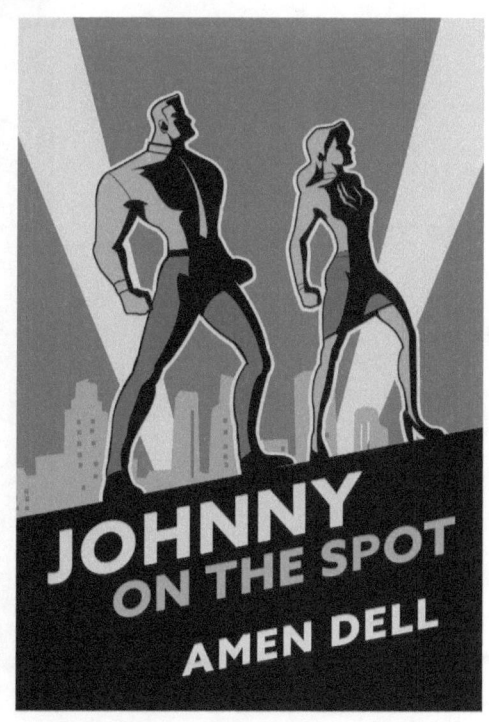

JOHNNY ON THE SPOT

AMEN DELL

CoachwhipBooks.com